My Own True Love?

My sailor hat flew off my head. Jeff ran to get it. What if he looked inside and saw what I had written about him? I would just die!

"You give that hat back to me right now, Jeff Davidson!" I cried.

Darlene and Suzy did their best to get the hat away from Jeff, but they were no match for him. Laughing as they chased after him, Jeff read the slogans from the hat out loud.

" 'To my best friend and fellow WHEBB club member.' WHEBB, huh? Must be some silly girls' club. And what's this here under the rim? 'My own true WHEBB love, Jeff Davidson!' "

He stopped short and stared at me.

I felt like sinking through the concrete. This was not how I planned to reveal my feelings at all!

We Hate Everything
But Boys

Linda Lewis

AN ARCHWAY PAPERBACK
Published by POCKET BOOKS • NEW YORK

AN ARCHWAY PAPERBACK *Original*

An Archway Paperback published by
POCKET BOOKS, a division of Simon & Schuster, Inc.
1230 Avenue of the Americas, New York, N.Y. 10020

ISBN: 0-671-53092-5

First Archway Paperback printing February, 1985

10 9 8 7 6 5 4 3 2 1

AN ARCHWAY PAPERBACK and colophon are
registered trademarks of Simon & Schuster, Inc.

Printed in the U.S.A.

To Lenny,
who gave me the strength
not to quit

We Hate Everything
But Boys

Chapter One

It was warm that first day of school. Hundreds of kids made their way toward the open doors of P.S. 373. I tripped over two of them in my rush to get there.

There are six grades in P.S. 373. Seven, if you count kindergarten. The reason that I was so anxious to start school was because I had finally made it to the top. I was a sixth-grader, and I was going to have the best year ever!

"Faster, Suzy," I urged. "I think I see HIM up ahead." HIM was Jeff Davidson, the most important boy in my life. Suzy Kletzel was my best friend, except for Darlene Mason.

Suzy was short and chubby, like a little ball of butter. Freckles were generously sprinkled

1

across her round, good-natured face. She was always giggling, always fun to be with. And then there was the fact that Suzy was lucky enough to live in Jeff's building. That certainly helped our friendship.

As I pushed through the crowds of kids, I held my class card tightly. It stated that my new class was 6-1, the same as Suzy's. I couldn't wait to find out if Jeff was going to be in my class again.

Last year he was in my class. I could have had a great time with him all year long. Unfortunately I didn't realize that boys were wonderful creatures until the last few months of school. As for Jeff, I didn't even know that I was crazy about him until that day in June.

We were playing basketball in the gym. He stretched out his foot as I dribbled the ball past him. The ball bounced away. I went sprawling on the floor, in front of the whole class!

"Clumsy!" he shouted.

I could have died of embarrassment!

"You did that on purpose, Jeff Davidson!" I began. Before I could say more, he reached out his hand to help me up.

I still remember how I tingled when I touched his hand! I looked up into his chubby face and shivered. I saw the cute way his hair

2

curled down onto his forehead. He shook his hair back from his face and grinned.

His teeth were so white! His eyes were so blue! I sat there in the middle of the gym, with my hand in his, staring into his eyes. Then I became aware of what was going on around me.

Marvin Haven, this creep from my block, had a big smirk on his face. I was tempted to go over and smack it. Harley Silver, the handsomest boy in our class, shouted, "That's love for you!"

Then it hit me. Love! Is that why my heart was beating so fast? Is that why his eyes burned through mine? Is that why my hand, still holding his, was sweating so?

I couldn't believe it! I, Linda Berman, was a tomboy. I had always made fun of giggly girls who swooned over the opposite sex. How could I have been struck with an emotion like love?

Impossible! Boys were great for kidding around with. They were fine for playing ball or trading baseball cards. But love! That was for those silly, frilly-type girls, not for me!

I shook my hand loose from his and rubbed my knee. Then I looked up at him again. He was still grinning! I couldn't keep my eyes off him. Who cared what the rest of the class thought?

That was it for me. From that time on I was as boy-crazy as any of the other girls. All we could think of was boys, boys, boys.

Anyhow, to get back to the first day of school, I was dying to see Jeff again. It was his head I had spotted. I would know that curly mop anywhere!

Forgetting Suzy, I shoved through crowds of crying kindergarteners, leaving their mothers for the first time. I pushed past the excited first-graders, and headed to the second grade line. There he was, placing his little sister with her class.

I stopped short. I didn't want to look like I was chasing after him. I had to look cool. I decided to pretend to be looking for my brothers, Ira and Joey. They were twins and also in the second grade. Of course I knew my mother hadn't gotten them to school yet.

"Where could they be?" I asked myself loudly.

He noticed me right away. "Hi, Berman! What are you doing in the second grade line? Did you get demoted or something?" Jeff was always making jokes. He grinned and my heart did flips.

I tried to look uninterested. "Oh, hi Jeff. Is this the second grade line? I was looking for my brothers."

4

I strolled over to where he was standing and smiled up at him. He was taller than I remembered—probably grew over the summer. My heart was hammering.

"Yeah, it's the second grade line, dummy." He shook back the curl that drooped in his eyes. "My sister's here, but I haven't seen your brothers. What class are you in this year, anyhow?"

"6-1. What about you?" I held my breath.

"I'm in 6-3. Birnbaum's the teacher. She's supposed to be real easy, so I feel good."

He felt good! Big deal, easy teacher. I wouldn't care who my teacher was if only I could be together with Jeff! 6-3 was Darlene's class. That lucky girl would be with Jeff and not even appreciate it!

Now the whole school year was ruined! Sadly I turned and saw Suzy waiting for me to join her.

"Well, see you around," I said. I smacked him across the backside with my looseleaf and went weaving through the crowd of kids.

"Why, you!" He dropped his sister's hand and started after me.

"Hey, Davidson. Stop that running here!" a deep voice boomed. It was Mr. Wohl, the principal, looking meaner than ever.

I walked innocently toward the sixth grade

5

Chapter Two

The sign we were looking for said 6-1, Room 409, Miss Delaney. Suzy and I looked at each other and groaned. Miss Delaney! Everyone knew about Miss Delaney. She was the strictest teacher in the whole school. And boy, did she make you work!

We got in line and looked to see who else was in our class. A few feet ahead of us stood Harley Silver and Kenton Wolfson, the two cutest boys in the sixth grade. When Suzy saw them, she poked me in the ribs and giggled. "Linda, what luck! Both Harley and Ken are in our class. Darlene will just die when she finds out!"

I nodded. "She sure will. Darlene felt bad

enough because she was separated from us this year. Wait until she hears that Harley and Ken are in our class, too."

"Oh no, Linda! Don't tell me that's Rena Widmark approaching our line!"

I looked at the girl walking toward us and groaned. "It is Suzy—old 'shapely-legs' Rena, in person."

Rena Widmark was the pushiest kid in our neighborhood. She thought every part of her was gorgeous, but she was particularly fond of her legs, which everyone else thought were fat. She would run her hands over them and brag, "Look at my shapely legs!"

Suddenly all whispering stopped. Miss Delaney was heading toward us, taking long, purposeful strides. She was tall and thin, with short gray hair. Spotting me talking to Suzy, Miss Delaney's gray eyes fixed mine with an icy stare. I quieted down immediately.

"Boys and girls! Quiet!" Miss Delaney's voice sounded like a foghorn. "I am Miss Delaney, your teacher this year. I want you to know that I will accept no nonsense from any of you. Let's start on the right foot by getting into a straight line immediately. And I mean perfectly straight. Then we will march silently up to our room."

Miss Delaney stood over us like an army

sergeant. We lined up just as she demanded. I hardly dared breathe, much less step out of line.

We started up the four long flights of steps. On the second floor landing, I heard snickering. I felt someone step on the back of my shoe. My foot slipped right out.

Who would dare give me a flat with Miss Delaney so close? I turned around quickly. There was Harley Silver with a grin plastered across his handsome conceited face!

Now I usually don't fall for overly handsome boys. They know they're good-looking and act too stuck-up. I, myself, am far from perfect in the looks department. I've got a decent enough figure and big blue eyes going for me. Unfortunately, my nose is on the big side too, definitely a minus.

Anyhow, back to Harley. I have to admit that Darlene, who is absolutely crazy about him, has good reason to be. He's dark, with deep brown eyes and black hair that flips over his forehead. He's also got a great body.

I couldn't resist giving his great body an elbow right in the stomach. That was for giving me the flat.

"Oof—that hurt!" he moaned.

I don't know what he would have done if we hadn't heard the clink of Miss Delaney's high heels approaching. We quickly straightened up and got back into line before she could notice that we were fooling around.

"I'll get you on the way home," he whispered when she had passed by.

I just smiled an innocent smile.

When we got to our room, Miss Delaney lined us up in size places.

"I believe in assigned seats," she stated. "I want you to sit four to a table. The smallest children will be at the front of the room. That way you can see me and I can see you!"

Suzy's a little taller than I am. She slouched down so that she could be behind me in line. Kenton Wolfson tried to stretch himself so that he could be in front of Harley. Poor Ken didn't quite make it. Miss Delaney spotted him. She separated him from Harley and stuck him right between Suzy and me! Suzy was bouncing with joy!

Harley was placed at the table behind us along with Rena Widmark, Jan Zieglebaum, and Lisa Finklestein. They all looked stunned and starry-eyed at being lucky enough to sit with handsome Harley.

Jan Zieglebaum was a nice shy kid. Her problem was that she was skinny and flat-chested. She looked about eight. Lisa Finklestein was one of those lucky girls born with everything. She had perfect features, skin, and hair. Her parents showered her with the latest clothes.

Darlene would flip when she found out who was sitting with Harley!

When we were all seated, Miss Delaney began to speak: "Boys and girls, you are most fortunate to be in class 6-1 this year."

Suzy and I looked at each other, and she began to giggle. Miss Delaney gave us an icy stare and went on.

"Because this is the top sixth grade class, you will have many wonderful experiences this year. Of course you will be responsible for the regular sixth grade work. In my class this includes nightly homework, weekly reports, and monthly major projects.

"This classroom also serves as the school library, so you will learn to catalogue and check out books. We will also order and distribute *The New York Times* and *Weekly Readers* for the rest of the school. I am given these responsibilities because," she puffed up her chest with pride, "I am the best teacher in the entire school. I expect you to do these jobs in a manner that will make me proud at all times!"

I couldn't stand it. I leaned across Ken and whispered to Suzy, "What did we do to deserve this?"

Just at that moment, Miss Delaney focused

her eagle eyes right on me. "You! You're talking again! Stand up and let me look at you!"

I felt like crawling under the desk. I stood up, just as she had asked, my head hanging down. My big mouth was always getting me into trouble.

"Look at me!" Miss Delaney bellowed. Painfully, I raised my eyes to meet hers. She looked like a gray-haired panther, ready to spring on a victim—me.

"Let's get something straight here right from the beginning. I will not tolerate anyone speaking while I am speaking! Keep that up and you'll have nothing but trouble this year! Do you understand me?"

"Y-Yes-s," I stammered.

"Yes, who?"

"Yes, Miss Delaney."

"That's better. Now sit down and keep quiet!"

Three o'clock found me standing outside the school with Suzy. We were waiting for Darlene's class to get out. I was miserable thinking about how Miss Delaney had made a fool out of me in front of the whole class.

Darlene came bounding out of school and rushed over to us, her long reddish hair swinging behind her.

"I had the most *exquisite* day," she announced. Darlene loves to use big words. I guess she thinks it makes her sound grown up. She looks a lot older than almost-twelve. She's tall and has already developed. I mean she has breasts, and a waistline, and hair under her arms. She even has her period!

"Mrs. Birnbaum is a real doll," she bubbled. "She let us sit next to our friends and talk if we kept the noise level down. And Linda, guess who's in my class—Jeff Davidson himself!"

"I know that already," I said sadly. "I saw Jeff this morning and he broke the news to me."

"Harley Silver and Kenton Wolfson are both in our class," informed Suzy.

"Both of them? Boy, are you lucky!" Darlene practically swooned. "I wonder where the boys are now?"

"Beats me," I answered. "Jeff and Harley both said they'd get me after school. But there's no sign of either of them. I guess they forgot."

We started walking home together. Darlene lived just one block from school. We usually left her at her corner, then Suzy and I walked to the next. There we split up and walked in opposite directions to our houses.

The part of New York City we lived in was called Washington Heights. All the houses were apartment buildings of five and six stories. There were enough kids in the neighborhood so that everyone walked to school. Going back and forth could be the nicest part of the day, if you ran into the right people. But today there were no boys in sight.

We were so busy telling each other the details of our school day that we didn't look where we were going. The first building we passed had a courtyard that was great for hiding. I was just saying how I had whacked Jeff with my looseleaf when I felt that very sensation across my backside!

I looked around and saw that it was Jeff! Harley and Kenton followed him out from where they had been hiding in the courtyard. They hadn't forgotten to get even with me after all! My backside hurt, but I felt great!

"Darlene, Suzy, help me!" I called. We all took off after the boys.

How I loved it! I loved being almost twelve. I loved liking boys. I loved to run down the city streets, my new loafers clacking on the sidewalk, the wind blowing across my face. I felt so alive!

I looked back and saw Darlene and Suzy losing ground as they ran after Harley and Ken. Suzy was so chubby, she waddled rather than ran. Darlene's sexy trot was hopeless!

I was getting to where I could almost grab Jeff. I reached out and went sprawling on the sidewalk. My looseleaf opened, sending papers all over the street.

Feeling very silly, I sat up. Jeff gathered up my papers and handed them to me. That maddening grin was spread over his face.

"See what happens when you mess with the wrong people," he teased. "Next time you'd better behave yourself."

"Next time it will be my turn to get you," I replied, brushing myself off.

Jeff ran down the block with Harley and Kenton. Suzy and Darlene had given up chasing them and were waiting for me by the entrance of Darlene's house. We decided to go up there.

Suzy called her mother to tell her where she was. Then I called mine.

"Hello, Ma?"

"Linda, where are you? Your brothers have been home for almost half an hour already!"

"I'm at Darlene's, Ma. Is it OK if I stay here awhile?"

"Is her mother home?"

"No, Ma. Darlene's mother works. She doesn't get home till five, but she doesn't mind if we're here."

"You know I don't like you to be all alone in someone's house with no supervision."

"I'm not alone, Ma. Darlene is here and Suzy is here, too. She already called her

15

mother, and she said OK. We're going to sit in Darlene's room, listen to records, and talk. Nothing will happen to us."

"What about your homework?"

"It's only the first day, Ma. I'll have plenty of time to do it after supper."

"Well, be sure you're home by 4:30."

"Sure, Ma." I hung up the phone with a sigh. One had to have such patience to deal with my mother. Both my parents were born in Europe. They were so old-fashioned, especially when compared to my friend's parents who were American-born. I always had to fight for the simplest things. Big deal if Darlene's parents weren't home!

We went into Darlene's room. She put on a record album. Darlene is just crazy about music and has tons of albums. In fact, Darlene has just about everything. Her room is big and looks out on the street. It's nicely decorated with a matching pink bedspread and ruffled curtains. On one wall she has pictures of rock singers. Under them is a stand for her record collection, stereo, and her very own TV.

What luxury! And Darlene has no brothers or sisters to share any of it with. Not like me. My apartment has only two bedrooms, so my brothers sleep in one and my parents sleep in the other. I got stuck in the living room. As far as music goes, all I ever get to listen to is the radio.

The song Darlene was playing was a sad one, all about breaking hearts. Darlene sighed deeply. "Life is so unfair! Why is it that you two are in Harley's class and I'm in Jeff's?"

"I know—it's just awful!" I agreed. "We have no control over our fate whatsoever. Some know-it-all principal like Mr. Wohl sticks us in a class and ruins our entire lives! Especially me—a whole year with Miss Delaney and without the boy I love!"

"Love!" giggled Suzy. "Do you really love Jeff Davidson?"

"Well, put it this way—I'm crazy about him! He's so cute in his lovable, chubby way. He's got a great sense of humor and is always doing something that makes me laugh. When he smiles, it just sends shivers through me!"

"Just looking at Harley sends shivers through me," said Darlene. "You know, I could actually live with not being in his class this year if only he would give me some little sign that he liked me. But he never does. It's awful!"

"I know just what you mean, Darlene," I agreed. "Sometimes I wonder if boys have feelings like girls do. All they seem to be interested in is playing ball and whether the Yankees beat the Tigers. The only thing they ever do with us is fool around."

"You're right, Linda. Boys seem incapable of having deep feelings like we do. But then again, maybe they do and just don't show it. I guess we'll never find out."

"Hey, maybe there is a way to find out!" I said, suddenly struck with a flash of brilliance. "We'll form a club—the WHEBB club!"

"What's that? Something to do with spiders?" Suzy said disinterestedly.

"Not web, silly—W-H-E-B-B. It's initials! It means We Hate Everything But Boys." I was so excited with my own idea that I couldn't sit still. I got up and opened Darlene's window. If I leaned out, I could see the park ball field where the boys were probably playing at that very moment.

I turned back to Darlene and Suzy. "We can have all sorts of secret club things. We can buy name buttons. On the back we'll have our secret boyfriend's name. On the front we'll write WHEBB in big letters. The boys will be dying to know what WHEBB means. But we won't tell them unless they let us know how they feel about us. It'll be so great!"

I could picture it all in my mind. Jeff would put his arm around me and say, "Linda, if I had only known how you felt about me sooner. I've wanted you for so long!"

"A club?" Suzy's voice brought me back to reality. "Do you think it will work?"

"Let's try it and see. We've got nothing to lose. Let's meet at my house on Saturday, walk down to the stores, and buy everything. The boys will probably be playing ball in the park. We'll drive them crazy when we show up wearing our WHEBB buttons!"

"Let's get sailor hats, too," Darlene suggested. "I've been meaning to buy one anyhow. We can print WHEBB across the front and get everyone to autograph them."

I plopped down on Darlene's pink bed. "I just can't wait for the weekend!"

Chapter Three

The first week of school seemed endless, but Saturday finally arrived. Darlene, Suzy, and I made our trip to the stores to buy our WHEBB club materials. Three weeks of allowance went to buy my name button and sailor hat. I sure hoped it would be worth it.

Each button had a printed name card. Darlene's said "Harley," Suzy's said "Ken," and mine said "Jeff." We turned these over and wrote WHEBB in big letters. Then we put the cards back in the buttons so all anyone could see was the word WHEBB.

Our sailor hats were printed with our names in the back and with WHEBB right in front.

Inside the rim, where no one could see, we wrote "My own true WHEBB love." Then we each wrote the name of our special boy.

We went to my house for our formal initiation. We sat on the hallway steps. That was the most private place I could offer, not having a room of my own.

I placed my hand on Suzy's head. "Suzanne Kletzel. Do you swear to spend all of your time and thoughts pursuing Kenton Wolfson and finding out how he feels about you?"

"I do," she giggled, covering her mouth.

"Then you are now an official member of WHEBB." I solemnly pinned on her button and placed her hat on her head. Suzy then repeated the ceremony for Darlene. Darlene did it for me. Our goals as WHEBB members were set!

The next step was to find the boys. On a beautiful fall Saturday, the place to look was the park baseball field. The trick was to get them to pay attention to us without being obvious.

"I'd just expire if Harley knew I was chasing after him," breathed Darlene.

"I know what we'll do," I suggested. "I'll get my ball, and we'll go play handball. The courts are right next to the baseball field. They'll have to notice us. Once they do, they'll be dying to know what our hats and buttons mean. Besides, we can use the exercise." I looked at Suzy's overstuffed body, and she giggled agreeably.

Stopping at my house for the ball was a mistake. As soon as my mother heard we were going to the park, she made me take my twin brothers along.

I didn't argue. I didn't want her to suspect the real reason we were going to the park. She thinks we're too young to be interested in boys.

Besides, Ira and Joey are kind of cute. No one else I know has twin brothers. Sometimes it's fun to walk down the street with them. People stop and say, "Oh look, twins!"

When we got to the park, I took a quick look over the stone wall that separated the ball field from the street. Sure enough, there were the boys! Jeff was pitching, Harley was first baseman, and Ken was playing right field.

"Perfect!" I whispered. "They're all on the right side of the field, close to the handball courts. They can't help but notice us."

We went into the park the back way. We walked to the courts, shouting and laughing. That was to make sure they knew that we were there.

"Ira! Joey!" I shouted, louder than I had to. "You go play on the back court. We'll play on the one over here."

My brothers gave each other a knowing look. They were glad to run off on their own.

We began to play. I swung hard and slapped the ball to Darlene. It bounced over her head and rolled right near first base. Harley was there concentrating on the batter.

"Ball, please!" Darlene shouted. Harley turned at the sound of her voice.

At that moment, Jeff threw an easy pitch to the batter. Smack! A line drive down first base! Harley was looking at us instead of the batter. The ball whizzed right past him.

By the time Ken picked it up, the runner was safe.

Harley was furious! "You dummy!" he yelled angrily at Darlene. "Look what you made me do!"

"Sorry," Darlene apologized sheepishly. She picked up the ball, her face beet-red. This was not going according to plan at all. But we were determined to try again.

Our next chance came when I aimed the ball perfectly. It bounced over Suzy's head to where Ken was standing.

"Go ahead, Suzy," I urged. "It's going right to him. Ask him to get the ball!"

Suzy stood there, giggling foolishly. "What if he gets mad?"

"So what if he gets mad? It's better than not noticing you at all!" I answered.

Suzy took a deep breath and waddled to the end of the court. "Oh Ken, could you get the ball for us, please?"

Ken glanced toward us. He gave the ball a kick in our direction.

"Gee, thanks." Suzy looked ready to swoon.

"Cut that out, Suzy," I said. "He didn't even care enough to bend over and pick up the ball. We've got to try something new."

The inning finally ended and Jeff's side went to bat. The boys all stood behind the batter's cage fooling around. It was time to make our next move.

"Darlene," I said. "How much gum did you buy at the store?"

"Six pieces. Two for each of us. Why?"

"Are you willing to sacrifice our gum for the purpose of getting the boys over here?"

Darlene nodded, a puzzled expression on her face.

"Good." I walked over to the back court and called, "Ira! Joey!"

"What is it, pest?" That was from Joey. He was the nastier of the two, without a doubt.

"How would you like some bubble gum?" I asked sweetly.

"What's the catch?"

"No catch at all. We'll give you each half a piece now for good will. All you have to do is go over to the batter's cage where Jeff, Harley, and Ken are standing. Chew your gum and let it be known that we have plenty more. If you can get the boys over here, we'll give you two extra pieces of gum for yourselves."

Bubble gum is a big deal to my brothers because my mother hardly ever lets us have it. Cavities and all that. So Ira and Joey were more than willing to give it a try. Sure enough, they returned in no time, Jeff, Harley, and Ken right behind them.

I took Ira aside. "What did you say to get them here so fast?"

"Not much. Just that you girls had some gum for them because you love them so much."

"Ira! I'll kill you! Why did you say something like that?"

"You wanted us to get them here, didn't you? Well, we got them!"

"That's right!" Joey added. "So put up and shut up!" He stretched out his grubby little hand.

I slammed down the rest of the gum. I stalked over to where Darlene and Suzy were talking to the boys. Darlene had already handed each of them a piece of gum.

Jeff spotted me and yelled, "Here comes another one!"

"As if they don't look dumb enough dressed

normally," Harley added. "They had to go out and get stupid name buttons and sailor hats!"

"I guess they got the sailor hats to match their bowed legs," Jeff laughed and slapped his own chubby thighs.

"It's cowboys who have bowed legs, not sailors," I corrected. This was great! They were paying attention to us, just as I had planned.

I saw Jeff staring at my button. "Hey, what does WHEBB mean, anyhow?" he asked, blowing a huge bubble with his gum.

"That's for us to know and you to find out!" I replied. I took the ball I had been holding and threw it at him playfully. I had meant to bounce it off his stomach. My aim was off and it hit him on the nose instead. The bubble burst and Jeff wound up with gum stuck all over his face.

Everyone laughed. He looked so silly.

Jeff tried to wipe the gum off his face. That just added dirt from his hands to the mess. The dirty gum smeared all over. Now he was getting mad.

Still, I couldn't resist giving him a dig. "Look at Jeff the jerk! He looks like a creature from outer space."

"Why, you!" he sputtered angrily. He started after me. "Help me get her, guys!" he called.

I turned around and ran, the three of them chasing after me. I glanced back at Jeff's face and was worried. He sure didn't look as if he was fooling around now!

I ran across the courts, hoping to reach the back exit of the park. The boys couldn't go too far from their game.

They were getting closer. I was beginning to run out of breath. I felt a sticky hand grab my arm.

"Don't hurt me, Jeff," I begged. "I didn't mean to get gum all over you."

"Too late for apologies now—get her guys!"

Harley grabbed me by my arms, and Ken grabbed me by my legs. They began swinging me from side to side over the hard concrete.

My sailor hat flew off my head. Jeff ran to get it. What if he looked inside and saw what I had written about him? I would just die!

Sure enough, Jeff picked up my hat and began to read.

"You give that hat back to me right now, Jeff Davidson!" I cried. But from my position dangling from my arms and legs, I was helpless.

Darlene and Suzy tried their best to get the hat away from Jeff, but they were no match for him. Laughing as they chased after him, Jeff read the slogans from the hat out loud.

" 'To my best friend and fellow WHEBB

club member.' WHEBB, huh? Must be some silly girls' club. And what's this here under the rim? 'My own true WHEBB love, Jeff David-son!' "

He stopped short and stared at me.

I felt like sinking through the concrete. This was not how I planned to reveal my feelings at all!

The world seemed to stop for a moment. Jeff just stood there, his face growing red. Darlene and Suzy both had their hands up to their open mouths. Harley and Ken loosened their grip on me as they stared at Jeff.

I took advantage of the moment to squirm out of their clutches. "Give me back my hat!" I demanded. "And you can just forget about what you read on it, too. That was just how I felt last week!"

This time Jeff didn't resist. He handed the hat back to me.

I walked to the courts where my brothers were watching the whole scene. My nostrils twitched as I fought to hold back the tears I felt building in my eyes.

Hearing screams from Darlene and Suzy, I turned around to find the boys now ganging up on them. Somehow, Jeff had managed to grab both Darlene's and Suzy's hats.

Jeff was laughing merrily. He tossed

Darlene's hat to Harley and Suzy's to Ken so they could read the truth for themselves.

Now Darlene looked about to cry. Suzy was giggling nervously while tears filled her eyes. I stood there helplessly, not knowing what to do.

"Hey, you guys! It's your turn to bat, Jeff!" I don't know what would have happened if Marvin Haven hadn't called the boys back to the game. They ran off to the batter's box, tossing our hats on the ground. They didn't even look back at us.

I felt positively humiliated. Not only had I ruined things for myself, but I had blown it for my friends as well.

"Let's go home!" I grabbed a brother in each hand.

We walked sadly back to my house, sniffling to hold back our tears.

"Boy, girls sure cry easily," Joey commented.

"Oh, shut up!" I snapped. I felt guilty for jumping on him that way. But at least my brothers kept quiet for the rest of the way home.

We sat on the hallway steps. The cool dampness of the hall seemed to close around us. It added to the feeling of gloom in the air.

Suzy's tears streaked the freckles of her

chubby cheeks. "How am I going to sit next to Ken at school after what he read? I'll never be able to face him again!"

"This whole thing has been a devastating experience," said Darlene. "You and your brilliant ideas, Linda!"

I tried to think. "Hey, let's look on the bright side of this!"

"What bright side?" asked Darlene.

I took a deep breath. I was nervous. I wanted to convince my friends things would be all right. But I also wanted to convince myself.

"Maybe," I said slowly, "once they think we like them, the boys might discover they like us. They have to be curious about WHEBB. They still don't know what it means. And because of WHEBB, we did get a lot of attention this afternoon."

"We didn't need that kind of attention!" Darlene scoffed. "It was humiliating. And now that they know we like them, the boys might not like us at all."

"But they don't know anything for sure!" I insisted. "After all, we have a right to change our minds! I told Jeff that what he read was just the way I felt last week. For all any of the boys know, we could like them today but not tomorrow."

30

"She's right, Darlene," Suzy dried the tears from her cheeks.

I smiled at her support. "What we have to do now is play it cool with them for a while. That'll confuse them. In the meanwhile, I'll think up another plan. WHEBB is not dead yet!"

Chapter Four

As planned, the WHEBB club members spent the next couple of weeks being cool to the boys. It really wasn't very hard to do. In fact, the boys made it easy for us. After school they kept out of our way. I guess they were embarrassed about what happened that day in the park too.

The first time I ran into Jeff I was so nervous I could hear my heart beating. He stopped short, mumbled "Hi," then turned and walked away. I was encouraged. It wasn't much, but it was a start.

In school, it was even easier to keep away from the boys. It was almost impossible to speak to anyone at all with old hawk-eye Delaney for a teacher. She had us in a strict routine that was never broken.

On arriving, we immediately went to work on our spelling assignment. While we worked, Miss Delaney sat at her desk and read *The New York Times*. But this didn't stop her from hearing everything that went on in the room. Anyone caught talking had to write each word ten times for homework.

After spelling, we did what was supposed to be social studies. Somehow, it seemed like half of this time was taken up each morning by Miss Delaney's telling us the story of her life. I already know that she lives with an older sister. She never married because there is no one good enough for her.

After social studies were English and language arts. Afternoons were for math and science. We never had any fun in Delaney's room. Never!

Then one day, Miss Delaney broke her usual boring routine. She got up in front of the room, smoothed her blouse across her chest, and announced that she actually wanted ideas from the class for a good language arts project. Then she waited for our replies.

There was dead silence in the room. Now that Miss Delaney finally gave us the chance to speak up, everyone was afraid to do so. We just stared blankly at one another.

The thought hit me that since Miss Delaney was so crazy about newspapers, a class newspaper would be a perfect project. But I didn't have the nerve to speak up. As Miss Delaney's eyes focused on me, my eyes dropped to the floor.

Then I heard a familiar nervous giggle. Shy Suzy was actually speaking! "I have an idea, Miss Delaney."

"Go ahead, Suzanne. Speak up so I can hear you."

Suzy swallowed. "How about if we wrote our own newspaper?"

Miss Delaney's expression didn't change. "Go on. What would you have in such a newspaper?"

"Well, uh," Suzy stammered. "How about—er—news from all the sixth grade classes? We can have results of the interclass ball games. We can have poems, stories, and artwork. We can even have a social column." Suzy giggled and the sound came out high-pitched and shrill. She clapped her hand over her mouth.

Miss Delaney stared at Suzy. She moved her eyes slowly over each one of us in turn. I was glad I hadn't said anything.

Then Miss Delaney actually began to smile. It had to be the first time she had smiled at anything besides her stories about herself. "A wonderful idea, Suzanne! You must be learning something from being in my class!"

Suzy beamed. I could have kicked myself now for not speaking up.

Miss Delaney continued. "We must have an editor. Tonight I want all who are interested to think up a format for our newspaper. Write it down and submit it to me tomorrow. The person who does the best format will be the editor."

I really wanted to be editor. For one thing, the job would bring lots of status. Also, the editor would probably get out of the room a lot to get news from the other classes. That would give me a chance to see Jeff during school.

I spent the whole night working on a format. I wrote a sample news story entitled, "Delaney Votes 'Yes' to Class Paper." I had a page for each of the items Suzy had mentioned. I even had sample artwork.

As for the social column, it was the perfect chance to publicize our WHEBB club. I called the column "What's Happening." I wrote: "What sixth grade boys, once misled by some writing on a sailor hat, are just dying to know the real meaning of the secret club, WHEBB?"

I went to bed thinking I had done a good job and would surely get to be editor. But the next morning brought me down to earth fast. I read

Suzy's format while we were walking to school. Hers was just as good as mine.

There were only five submissions of newspaper formats. Ken was the only boy who had bothered except for Steven Warshinsky. As the class brain, he was hardly qualified to be a boy. Suzy, Jan Zieglebaum, and I were the only girls.

That morning, while we were doing spelling, Miss Delaney read our formats instead of *The New York Times*. I kept looking up at her, watching her expression. Once I saw her smirk. I tried to see what paper had created that response. I could see nothing.

The morning dragged worse than ever. I was dying to know if I had made editor. Finally Miss Delaney stood up, tucking in her blouse.

"Boys and girls! Your attention! My search for the editor of our paper has ended. Come to the front of the room when I call your name."

It seemed to take forever until she called anyone. My heart was hammering. How I wanted to be editor.

"Linda Berman!" When I heard my name, I stood up so quickly that I knocked my chair to the floor. Everyone laughed.

"Yes, Miss Delaney." I tried to pick up my chair with dignity. I only succeeded in banging it against the table.

"Linda! Didn't you hear me? Come to the front of the room!"

I managed to get there without banging into anything else. I stood there proudly. I was ready to receive my praise for having written such a great format.

But Miss Delaney ignored me and went right on calling names. "Suzanne Kletzel. Steven Warshinsky. Kenton Wolfson. Jan Zieglebaum." She called everyone who had written a format.

She looked us over. "Well boys and girls, it was a difficult job for me to chose the best of your formats. But after careful consideration, I have decided on the editor—Steven Warshinsky!"

I groaned. Steven Warshinsky, of all people. At least if it had been Suzy, she would have deserved it for coming up with the idea. But Steven Warshinsky! Just like Miss Delaney. She probably picked him just because he was a boy and her favorite!

Miss Delaney rambled on. "Of course being editor is such a big job that even Steven will need help. Therefore, I have made each of you associate editors. Kenton, you are sports editor. Suzanne, you are art editor. Jan, you are creative writing editor. And Linda," she sighed. "I guess you can be social editor!"

Social editor! In a way, that was even better than being editor-in-chief! This was my big chance! The perfect opportunity to interview THE BOYS. I walked back to my seat in a daze.

I could just picture myself in the schoolyard. I'd go up to Jeff and say, "I'm here as the official representative of our school newspaper. As social editor, I must know the name of the girl you like best."

He would be too impressed to resist. He would stare into my eyes and say, "Linda, it's you. It's always been you."

"Linda. Linda?"

Back to reality. The class had begun the day's math lesson and Miss Delaney was calling on me to answer the next question. I had no idea which one!

Frantically, I looked around the room for help. Suzy came to my rescue. Secretly she pointed to question number three.

I took a deep breath and answered the question. Miss Delaney went on to someone else.

Now I was safe from being called on for a while. I could sit and formulate my plans. How could I use my new position as social editor to further the goals of WHEBB?

Chapter Five

I got my first shot at a great scoop for "What's Happening" just a few weeks later. It was the time of year when one's brains turned to baseball. For one thing, the World Series had begun. As usual, the New York Yankees were playing again. Living in New York, either you loved the Yankees or you hated them. Being a Mets fan myself, I belonged to the group that hated the Yankees. They were such a conceited team!

Miss Delaney was a Yankee fan. She was so gung ho that she actually allowed us to bring a radio to school to listen to the final World Series game. I was overjoyed when the Yankees went down to defeat.

We couldn't let the time of year go by without having our own P.S. 373 World Series. There were qualifying games after school. One class after another was eliminated. The two best would fight it out in a best-two-out-of-three match.

As things turned out, 6-1 and 6-3 were the two classes in the playoffs. The rivalry ran high. Boy, was I torn apart!

On one side was my own class. On the other side was Jeff's. Darlene was in the same situation as I was, only in reverse. Harley was the captain of her class's rival team.

We had split the first two games. We were down to the one that would decide the championship. Everyone was coming to the schoolyard at 3:30 for this game. Everyone, that is, but Suzy Kletzel. She had the misfortune of having an orthodontist appointment for that very afternoon. She was having braces put on her teeth.

Suzy tried everything to get her appointment changed, but her mother stood firm. Poor Suzy, it was terrible enough to get braces. But to have to miss the game!

So it was just Darlene and I who walked together to the game that afternoon. We had on our WHEBB buttons and sailor hats. We also had on sweaters because the October winds blew chilly.

Under my arm was my little notepad entitled, "Facts for What's Happening." That was just in case I overheard any interesting "happenings" while at the game.

Darlene sighed deeply as we walked. "Why is life so devastatingly unfair? It would have been so much simpler if Harley had been in my class and Jeff in yours."

"I know just what you mean, Darlene," I answered. "I feel like such a fool at these games. One moment I'm jumping up and cheering for my class. Then Jeff gets up and I'm cheering for him. I wind up getting dirty looks from everyone. Sue-Ann Fein even told me that I should transfer out of our class and into hers!"

"Sue-Ann Fein? Don't pay any attention to her. She'd just die if you were in her class. The way she's always flirting with Jeff!"

"I know," I said glumly. "And I bet he flirts right back with her when I'm not around."

Sue-Ann Fein was a bouncy outgoing person. She never seemed to care about being *obvious* when she flirted with Jeff. In fact, I think she enjoyed rubbing in the fact that she was in his class and I wasn't. I bet she flirted with him even more in front of me! And there was nothing I could do about it. Yes, life was unfair.

As we approached the schoolyard, I felt my

heartbeat quicken. The boys were already there, warming up. The girls were there too, swarming over the steps that led down to the schoolyard. We used them as bleachers for our games.

Jeff was practicing pitching. He wore a light blue tee shirt with his jeans, and brand new sneakers that made his feet look too big. He tossed the curls out of his eyes. As his eyes met mine, he sort of half smiled. Then he went back to pitching.

That smile went right through me. I knew things were all right between us again.

"There's Harley playing shortstop. Doesn't he look scrumptious?" Darlene's voice squeaked with excitement.

"Scrumptious? Well, he does look cute," I admitted. Harley had rolled up his white tee shirt to show off his dark skin. His arms were starting to get some gorgeous muscles.

"Oh drat!" I whispered to Darlene as we approached the steps. "There's that pushy Sue-Ann."

"Be grateful that there's only one other Jeff-fan here," she whispered back. "Harley's got an entire cheering section! There's Jan Ziegle-baum, Lisa Finklestein, and Rena Widmark, all sitting there swooning over him. I never have Harley to myself!"

We arrived right in the middle of an unbelievable conversation centering around Rena Widmark. I heard her husky voice saying proudly, "Now that I'm almost twelve, my mother has finally agreed to get me a bra! I just can't wait!"

"Well, if you're going to get a bra, I'm going to get one too," stated Lisa, shaking her lovely blond hair. "My mother gets me whatever I want."

I looked at Rena's body and then at Lisa's. Sure enough, they both had small bumps in their shirts. I wasn't impressed. There wasn't enough for either of them to need a bra. In fact, I had more than they did. And I had no desire to wear a bra until I really had to. You have to take too much teasing.

Of all of us girls, Darlene was the only one who wore a bra. She was always being teased because of it. Even now, she looked away uncomfortably while Rena rambled on.

"My mother is taking me to Alexander's department store this very weekend. They sell these bras that grow right with you. And I certainly expect to keep right on growing!" She laughed viciously. "Of course I'm not going to overdo it. I don't want to be huge, like Darlene!"

Boy, was Rena disgusting. I looked over at

Darlene. She was staring over at the boys as if she didn't even hear our conversation. Only her blushing-red face showed me that she really did.

"Why don't you shut up already, Rena?" I said. "I've already got all the facts I need about your bra. You'll read about it in 'What's Happening.'"

"Besides, the game is starting. I'd rather watch the boys than talk about your bra," said Lisa.

Rena gave me a dirty look. But she shut up and began watching the game.

Ken was the first one up for our side. Poor Suzy would have loved to see him as he belted Jeff's pitch for a double. Jeff got the next two batters out, and then Harley was up.

Now I was really torn. I wanted Harley to hit the ball and score for our team. I also wanted Jeff to strike him out. That part won out.

"Strike him out, Jeff!" I yelled.

"Traitor!" sneered Rena Widmark. "You ought to be expelled from our class!"

Whack! The bat connected with the ball. It went whizzing out to right field. The right fielder went running after it. By the time he picked it up, Ken had already scored and Harley was on his way home.

My class cheered wildly. All except me. I

could see Jeff's poor dejected face. He hung his head and scraped his foot across the pitcher's mound.

"Yeah, Harley! Yeah, Ken!" The shouts from all the girls finally got to them. The two heroes approached the steps so they could be further admired. Both of them were panting to show how hard they had worked scoring their runs.

"Anyone have any gum?" was the first comment from Harley, the hero. He held out his hand.

"Here, Harley!" Rena and Lisa fought to give him pieces of gum. He took them both and tossed one over to Ken.

"I've got some turkish taffy. Want some?" Darlene asked as she smiled sexily at Harley.

"Yeah, I'll take some." He put the gum in his pocket and sat down next to Darlene, helping himself to three pieces of taffy.

Lisa, Rena, and Jan all shot dirty looks in Darlene's direction. It didn't matter. She only had eyes for Harley.

"We're really whipping your class's hide," he grinned at Darlene.

"That ain't no way to talk to a lady," a deep voice interrupted. "Move over, boy. Let a *real man* show you how to operate."

The *real man* shoved Harley aside and took his place next to Darlene. He had a fat friend with him who sat down too. Everyone's eyes focused on the two of them with horror.

The intruders were Roger Hall and Georgie Johnson. They were the two worst bullies in the sixth grade. They had been left back twice and were older and bigger than the rest of us.

Darlene shuddered with fear. Harley backed away sheepishly. "I was just leaving anyhow, man," he said. He ran off onto the field. What a chicken! It was sad to see that even the great Harley wouldn't mess with Roger and Georgie.

Roger was tall and muscular. He wore his tee shirt rolled up to his shoulder with a pack of cigarettes stuck in his sleeve. His dirty-blond hair was greased back over his jug-handled ears. He had pimples all over his face.

Georgie was big, fat, dark, and greasy. He looked as if he could take two of our boys at once and crush them with his bare hands.

Roger moved closer to Darlene. "What's the matter with you, baby? Givin' away your candy like that. With me around you won't have to give nothin' to none of these punks. In fact, I've got somethin' to give you!"

Darlene tried to slide away from him, but she was already on the edge of the steps. "I don't want anything, thank you."

"Aw, don't hold back, baby. With a body like yours, you must be dyin' for a real man. Relax. I'll show you what a good time really is." He put his pimply arm around her and pulled her close to him.

Darlene was absolutely white. I wanted to help her, but I was scared to death.

I ran behind the safety of the fence. "Jump under the railing," I whispered loudly.

Darlene just sat there as if she couldn't move. Then she gave Roger a sharp jab with her left elbow and slid under the railing. She jumped down to the concrete schoolyard, got her balance, and ran up into the street. There I joined her.

We ran up the block as fast as we could. We were sure they would follow us. We could hear them yelling after us, "Go baby, go! Shake it up baby! Look at that wiggle!"

"Slow down, Darlene," I panted as we got to the corner. "They're not following us."

I looked at Darlene, and she had tears streaking her face. She just shook her head and kept walking. Unsure of what to do, I just followed her. She walked so fast that I had to run to keep up with her.

We walked up the five flights of stairs to her apartment. She opened the door with her key and went straight to her room. She plopped face down on her bed. She cried and cried as if she'd never stop.

I was very uncomfortable. I didn't know if she wanted me to go or stay. No one was home in her house as usual. I didn't feel I should leave her alone, so I just sat next to her.

Finally, her sobs slowed down. "Oh, Linda," she moaned. "I'll never be able to face the kids again! Did you hear the names Roger called me?"

"Aw, Darlene, everyone knows that Roger and Georgie are the dumbest things around. No one cares what they say."

"Well, I care! And it's not just what *they* said, either. Do you remember what Rena Widmark said about my body when we first got to the schoolyard?"

"I remember. But she's an idiot, too. She's just jealous because Harley pays more attention to you than he does to her."

"Maybe he does. But I never know whether he's interested in me or in my breasts. That's the way it is with me and boys!"

"It is?" I asked.

"Yes," she said, sniffling. "And it's awful! Do you realize that I've had my period since I was nine years old? Here I am, not even twelve, and I'm as big as my mother! I always feel that people are staring at me as if I'm some sort of freak. And high school guys ask me out just because they think I'm an easy mark!"

"They do?"

"Yes." Darlene nodded. "Like last year, when I went with my mother to visit one of her old friends. She has a son who's a high school senior. He invited me to his room to listen to some records while our mothers had coffee." Darlene reached for a tissue and blew her nose.

"Go on, go on."

"Well, before I knew it, he pushed me down on the bed and he grabbed my breasts!"

"Wow! What did you do?"

"I screamed and jumped off the bed. Our mothers came running into the room. I made some sort of excuse about having banged my foot into the dresser."

"Did you tell your mother what had happened?"

"No. I was too ashamed. You're the first one I told about any of these things. Everyone else thinks it's great to be big like this. But I—I hate it!" Darlene blew her nose hard. "You won't tell anyone, ever, will you?"

"Of course not, Darlene," I promised. "But think of things this way. Wouldn't you rather be big than totally undeveloped like Jan Zieglebaum? No boys pay her any attention at all."

"I guess so," she admitted.

"And you heard Rena and Lisa. They just can't wait to have enough to fill out a bra!"

"Do you really think so, Linda?"

"Of course! Besides, everyone's starting to develop now. Soon you won't seem to stick out at all!"

Chapter Six

Jan Zieglebaum was having a party, the first party of the school year. Unfortunately this party was only for girls. The WHEBB club wasn't happy about that at all.

I tried hard to convince Jan to invite the boys, but it wasn't that she didn't want them there. The problem was her mother—she thought we were too young for a party with boys!

Jan's parents are even worse than my parents. They are not only old-fashioned, but religious. They told Jan that it's sinful to even hold hands with a boy until you're engaged. Since Jan was so young, just turning eleven while the rest of us were pushing twelve, they certainly weren't going to give in.

So Saturday found me dressed up at an all-girls party.

It started out very slow. We stood around for a while in Jan's living room, talking and giggling. Mrs. Zieglebaum hovered around us. Finally, she decided to get the party rolling.

"Let's have a lovely game of Pin the Tail on the Donkey!" she suggested cheerily.

Darlene and I looked at one another. "No self-respecting WHEBB member would be caught playing Pin the Tail on the Donkey," I whispered to her. "Let's go hide in the bathroom!"

We looked around for Suzy. There she was at the refreshment table, happily sticking potato chips into onion dip.

I walked over and grabbed her arm. "Suzy! Stop eating! We're having a WHEBB meeting in the bathroom. Right now!"

"Whmpf?" Suzy tried hard to swallow.

"Never mind why. Just follow us in there fast!"

Too late. Mrs. Zieglebaum had spotted us. She headed toward us with three tails in her outstretched hand. "Hurry up girls, or you'll lose your turn. You've the last three numbers."

"Thank you, Mrs. Zieglebaum." I took tail number eight. I tried my best to smile sweetly.

Rena Widmark won the prize. It was a pair of nail clippers—just the right thing for her shapely toenails.

"We've got to do something to liven up this party!" I groaned to Darlene.

"I have an idea," she said. She stood up, towering over the rest of the girls. "Hey, girls," she announced. "I brought some of my records with me. Let's practice dancing."

"Great idea, Darlene," I seconded.

Mrs. Zieglebaum looked nervous.

"Okay with you, Mom?" Jan asked timidly.

She hesitated. "Well, I guess so. If you don't make too much noise."

"We won't." Jan put on a record. We paired off and began practicing our fast dance steps.

But even dancing isn't much fun when there are just girls around. I soon tired of this as well.

I stopped dancing. "Darlene, I just can't take this anymore—dancing and playing silly games with silly girls. We should be doing something to further our WHEBB goals!"

"Like what?"

"Like making some phone calls to the boys. Isn't that the kind of thing members of WHEBB would do to liven up an all-girls party? Let's get Suzy!"

Suzy was dancing with Jan. "Hey, Jan," I interrupted. "How would you like to have the next best thing to having the boys at your party?''

"What's that?"

"That's their voices on the telephone."

"What do you mean?" Boy, Jan could be thick!

"I mean we'll call them up. On the telephone. We'll disguise our voices. They won't even know it's us!"

Ignoring the terrified expression on Jan's face, I propelled her toward her parents' bedroom, where I knew there was a phone. Suzy and Darlene followed us in. I shut the door behind us.

"Whom shall we call first?" I asked.

"Well, considering that this is your idea, Linda," said Darlene. "Why don't you go first and call Jeff?"

"Okay. I'll show you I'm not chicken." I picked up the phone and dialed Jeff's number. I had it memorized. My heart beat rapidly as I heard the ringing of his phone. I had no idea what I was going to say if he picked it up!

"Hello?" A woman's voice answered.

"Hello." My voice shook. Stupid me! I hadn't thought that his mother might answer. "Mrs. D-D-Davidson?"

"Yes. Who is this?"

"You don't know me, Mrs. Davidson," I said in my best imitation of a southern accent.

"Ah just had to tell you that Ahm in love with yo' son!"

I slammed down the phone. There was dead silence in the room. I felt like I had made a fool out of myself. I looked down at the floor.

Then I heard Suzy's giggle. The others began to laugh, too.

"That was great, Linda!" Suzy said enthusiastically. "Now call Ken!"

"Who, me? Why don't you call him, Suzy?"

"Oh, I don't have the nerve to do that. I'd start giggling and he'd know it was me right away. You do it, Linda. You're so good at these calls!"

I was always a softy for Suzy. I also loved the attention I was getting from my friends. So, even though I knew what I was doing really wasn't right, I dialed the number she gave me.

"Wolfson's TV repair," a deep voice answered.

I put on my most grown-up sounding voice. "Yes. I'm having trouble with my TV. Could you send someone to look at it?"

"What does your problem seem to be, Ma'am?"

Ma'am! He believed me! I took a deep breath. "It's the—uh—the picture! I get no picture at all."

"There's a minimum charge for a service call."

"That's all right." I was starting to feel secure now. "Just send the man to 379 Ft. Washington Avenue. That was Jeff's address. It's apartment 1B. And, by the way, Mr. Wolfson."

"Yes?"

"I happen to know your son, Kenton. He's such a lovely young boy!" Barely able to keep from laughing, I hung up the phone. I looked to see if my efforts had been appreciated.

They were. All the girls were rolling with laughter. Darlene was holding her stomach, and Suzy had tears rolling down her face. Jan was kicking her feet on the bed.

Now I was really enjoying myself. I didn't want to think about the fact that what I was doing was wrong.

"Try Harley next," Darlene begged when she got back her voice. "Maybe he's home now."

"Sure!" After the terrific way I had handled Mr. Wolfson, I was ready to call anyone. I reached for the phone.

"What's going on here? What are you girls doing?"

I looked up. Mrs. Zieglebaum was standing by the door. Did she look mad! We had been laughing so hard, we never heard her come in.

"N-nothing!" I stammered.

"What do you mean, nothing? Closing yourselves away from the party like this and using the phone! Jan, you come over here this instant. I want you to tell me exactly what is going on."

Jan walked meekly over to where her mother stood. "N-nothing's going on, M-Mom. We were just having some fun."

"Fun! If this is your idea of fun, you can expect it to be your very last birthday party. Now you just tell me whom you were calling and why!"

Jan hung her head. "Well, er—we wanted to—we tried—it was just for fun, Mom, really it was!" Tears began running down her cheeks.

The ice cream I had eaten churned in my stomach. I knew it was my fault that Jan was in trouble.

I took a deep breath. "Mrs. Zieglebaum. Jan didn't do anything. I was the one who made the calls."

"And whom were you calling?" she asked icily.

"Just some boys from school. But we didn't even get a chance to speak to them, just their parents. We didn't say much."

"In that case, what was that about having a TV repaired?"

Now I was really stuck. That sneaky Mrs. Zieglebaum must have been listening to everything we said! I had to admit the whole thing. I felt so guilty. I wished I could drop through the floor and disappear.

Mrs. Zieglebaum glared at me. "Don't you realize how terrible it would have been if Mr. Wolfson had gone out of his way to get that TV set? The man has a business to operate. I want you to call him up right now and apologize!"

Everyone was looking at me sympathetically. Except for Jan. She was looking at the floor. But none of my friends could help me. I had to do this alone. One look at Mrs. Zieglebaum's face told me I had no choice but to make the call.

Slowly, I dialed Ken's number again. My stomach did flip-flops as the ringing began.

"Wolfson's TV repair."

"Is this Mr. Wolfson?"

"Yes. Who is this?"

"You don't know me, Mr. Wolfson. I'm a girl from Ken's class. We're at a party and trying to have some fun. We made some calls, and er, well—I made that last call to you. I know I shouldn't have, so just don't come to that address because it's Jeff's, and there's no broken TV, and I'm sorry, and—well, goodbye!"

Mrs. Zieglebaum's face softened slightly. "That's better. Now go back to the rest of the party. We're about to have a nice game of musical chairs." She led us back to the living room.

I sighed with relief. At least she wasn't making me call Mrs. Davidson!

I was very quiet for the rest of the party. I played musical chairs and hot potato, just as I had at parties when I was little. I danced with Rena Widmark in the dance contest and won a tiny teddy bear as a prize.

When the party was over, I thanked Mrs. Zieglebaum for having me. I said I was sorry for that *little problem.*

I really was sorry. I had made a fool of myself in front of everyone. I had been a nuisance to the boys' parents, especially Mr. Wolfson. And how was I going to face Ken in school when he found out?

It was a sad fate for a charter member of the WHEBB club!

Chapter Seven

No one knew where the rumor started. Soon everyone was whispering that the school was having a dance for Valentine's Day. The WHEBB club got right to work thinking of ways to get the boys to ask us to the dance.

I decided to use "What's Happening" for our purposes. Therefore, the pre-Christmas issue had the headline, "Valentine's Dance Planned for Sixth Grade." The article advised each boy to ask his favorite girl before someone else did. I was determined to get Jeff to ask me before school let out!

The last week before Christmas vacation is always unreal. It was impossible to concentrate on schoolwork when Christmas and Chanukah decorations were plastered all over the room.

Miss Delaney didn't make it any easier for us. She spent the mornings giving us boring details of how she and her sister were putting up their tree. It was the best in the neighborhood, of course. So was their famous eggnog. They always had a batch on hand for friends who might drop in. It was hard to believe that Miss Delaney actually had friends!

We girls had a break from the usual routine on the Tuesday before vacation. We had the day off from school so we could go and take the Huntington test. Huntington is an all-girls school downtown in New York City. It's only for bright kids. You need to have a high I.Q. and to pass a test to get in. Those who passed the test could go to Huntington the next year instead of the neighborhood junior high school, 515.

About ten girls met in front of the park that morning, waiting for the bus to take us downtown.

"Brr, it's cold," I shivered, jumping from one foot to the other to keep warm. "Winter has definitely set in."

"I don't know what I'm doing here anyhow," stated Darlene. "There's no way I could last in a school that isn't coeducational."

"What does that mean?" asked Rena.

61

"It means no boys," I informed. "And it's worth a trip downtown to get away from Miss Delaney for a day."

The bus finally pulled up. We took the long trip through the city. I felt very grown-up riding downtown without any adults. We had been carefully schooled in how to get there. We got off by Central Park. We walked the three long blocks to Huntington in one chattering group.

I hung back from the others and took in the city around me. The buildings were so tall that it made me dizzy to look up at the tops. Each building had a doorman and was decked in Christmas splendor. Everyone in this neighborhood must be rich, I thought. It was all so strange to me. I felt as if I didn't belong here at all. Suddenly, I wasn't sure if taking the Huntington test was worth a day off from Delaney.

The gray winter sky hung over the tall buildings. The chill wind roared off Central Park and lashed right through my winter coat. I shivered and ran to catch up with the others.

I walked close to Darlene as we approached the building that was Huntington. It was big and gray and full of arched windows, towers, and carvings. It was old and scary, not at all like P.S. 373. As I walked up the steps, I felt as if I was approaching a deep, dark cave. It was a frightening feeling.

"This is Gothic architecture," Darlene whispered to me as we struggled to open the heavy doors.

"I don't care what you call it," I frowned. "This place is ugly. I don't like it at all."

But the inside of Huntington, at least, was a lot cheerier than the outside. The walls were painted a sunny yellow, and artwork hung in the halls.

There were girls standing in the halls to help us. They were all very friendly. They told us how much they liked it at Huntington and how good the teachers were. Then they went out of their way to help us find our test-taking rooms.

We had been assigned rooms alphabetically. My room was for names beginning with letters A through F. The only one of my group who was with me was Lisa Finklestein. Having her there was worse than having no one at all.

She looked so calm and collected as she leafed through her test booklet. One hand smoothed her beautiful hair. Just watching her being calm made me nervous.

Nervous! That was an understatement. I could see right away that this test was hard. I tried going through it fast, skipping over the questions I didn't know. I planned on going back and finishing them at the end. But there was so much I wasn't sure of! I blackened the little spaces on the answer sheet as best I could.

I shifted in my seat uncomfortably. The desk was the kind with a little arm for writing attached to one side. I was used to the big tables in Miss Delaney's room where I could spread out all my papers. I didn't have enough room to do that here. As I shifted, I knocked my test booklet to the floor.

I never knew paper could make so much noise! Everyone turned to stare at me. The teacher in charge frowned in a manner that reminded me of Miss Delaney.

Miss Delaney, I thought, as I bent to pick up my booklet. If I could handle a year with Miss Delaney, I could handle anything. It was dumb to get nervous about a silly old test. Especially when I didn't really want to go to Huntington anyhow.

I picked up my test booklet as quietly as I could. I took a deep breath and went back to work.

When the test was over, our group gathered outside the building. I was anxious to hear what everyone else thought of Huntington and the test.

"I wonder where they got those questions from anyhow," grumbled Suzy.

"Even I didn't know half those vocabulary words," admitted Darlene.

"It was the hardest test I ever took," I said glumly.

"Oh, I don't know about that," Rena Widmark said. "They always throw some hard questions in tests like this to make you think it's worse than it really is. I thought I did rather well, myself."

"Me, too," said Lisa, tossing her hair. "And I'm sure I'd fit in here at Huntington just beautifully. The girls I spoke to today were all quality types. And this neighborhood just reeks of class. I can't wait to go here!"

"Well, that's just great to know," I replied. "Now we won't feel guilty thinking of you down here at Huntington while we're having fun at 515 with the boys!"

Lisa stuck her tongue out at me. "You're just saying that because you did lousy on the test, Linda. That's what they call sour grapes!"

"That's what you think, Lisa! It just so happens that no WHEBB club member would be caught dead in a school without boys!"

But even as I said this, I knew Lisa was right. It was sour grapes. As much as I disliked the feeling of coming downtown to the great big city, I still wanted to make Huntington. I couldn't stand the thought that beautiful perfect Lisa or old shapely-legs Rena might pass the test and I wouldn't!

Once we got back to school, it was easy to put Huntington out of my mind. After all, Christmas vacation was coming. Ten glorious days of freedom—freedom from school! We couldn't wait for the week to end. And I still had the Valentine's dance to think about. How could I get Jeff to ask me to go?

I didn't get to see Jeff at all until the last day of school before Christmas vacation. Traditionally, that day was always a fun day at school. Even Miss Delaney had enough sense not to give us our usual workload that day.

In the morning, the sixth grade had an assembly. Mrs. Birnbaum's class put on the holiday play. The auditorium was all decorated with Christmas trees and Chanukah menorahs. Mrs. Birnbaum, a sprig of holly pinned on her dress, sat proudly at the piano. She played holiday music as her class marched in and took their places on the stage.

I had a prime seat on the aisle. I nudged Suzy as Jeff waddled by. He was all dressed up in a Santa Claus costume.

"Boy, they really picked the right one to play Santa," I commented. "Jeff's getting so fat that he hardly needs a pillow."

"And look who they picked for Mrs. Claus!"

I looked and my stomach sank. It was Sue-Ann Fein! I watched the play with a growing sense of horror. There was constant contact between Mr. and Mrs. Claus. I counted three separate times that he put his arm around her. I felt sicker each time.

The worst moment was at the end. Jeff kissed Sue-Ann on both cheeks and said, "Baby, you're the greatest wife a man could ever hope for!"

Jeff looked as if he was really enjoying himself. Sue-Ann was just beaming. The thought of how many times they must have practiced that kissing scene was too much for me to bear. Why wasn't it me up there with him?

The play was over. The actors filed out of the auditorium. I slumped in my seat miserably, not wanting to look at anyone. Sue-Ann walked by me with her nose in the air. When she reached my seat, she quickly stuck out her tongue so no one would see but me. Then she smiled and strutted down the aisle.

There was no way that I could enjoy our class party that afternoon. Seeing Jeff kissing Sue-Ann had put me in a terrible mood, And knowing that he was probably dancing with her at their class party at that very moment didn't help at all.

Our party was a real dud, too. We had all the

tables and chairs pushed back to make a dance floor, but no one was dancing.

Maybe it was Miss Delaney's presence that made them too chicken to ask us to dance. At any rate, the boys all gathered at one end of the room like a flock of pigeons. They clowned around and stuffed their faces with Christmas candy.

The girls hovered around the opposite end, giggling and gossiping. Lisa Finklestein was busily bragging about her vacation plans.

"Do you know where I'm going over Christmas?" She twirled her gorgeous hair in her fingers. "To Florida! We're flying down tomorrow. We're staying in a first class hotel on the beach! I'll be getting a marvelous tan and meeting all sorts of cute boys. I just can't wait!"

It made me sick! I sat, wrapped in self-pity. I couldn't wait till school was over.

We took our time walking home from school that afternoon. We were standing on Darlene's corner in a big group. I saw Jeff approaching out of the corner of my eye. I pretended not to see him. I acted like I was fascinated by Lisa's repeating her news about her Florida trip.

"Well, if it isn't Santa," Harley interrupted. "Ho-ho-ho!"

"Wasn't that a great play our class put on today?" Jeff beamed.

"Everything was perfect, except for Santa Claus," teased Darlene. "He was too fat!"

"I bet you enjoyed Mrs. Santa. You looked so cute kissing each other," Rena said. I shot her a dirty look.

"Yeah, that Sue-Ann is a good kisser," Jeff smirked. "And not a bad dancer either. We had quite a party this afternoon."

I began getting that sinking feeling in my stomach again. "So you had a party this afternoon, too?" I managed to say.

"Yeah, and it was great! That Sue-Ann can really move—Why she almost dances better than I do!" he said with a teasing laugh.

His teasing was not what I wanted to hear. "I bet anyone dances better than you do," I snapped. "You can barely walk straight!"

He shrugged his shoulders and grinned. "Too bad you feel that way, Linda. Just when I was going to ask you to go to the Valentine's dance, too." He laughed and began walking away.

Now I was furious. "Well you can just ask Sue-Ann to go to the dance since she's so great! In fact you should both come in those silly Santa Claus outfits!" I shouted after him.

Darlene pulled me aside before I could say

more. "Shut your mouth before you put your foot in it any further, you dummy! He'll never ask you to the dance now. Look how you embarrassed him in front of all these kids!"

"I know," I wailed. "Me and my big mouth!"

On New Year's Eve, my parents did a very rare thing. They let me sleep over at Darlene's house! Her parents were going to a party next door. Darlene wanted me to keep her company. Mrs. Mason told my mother that she would look in to make sure we were all right. So my mother agreed to let me go.

It was almost time for me to leave. I was lying on my bed, trying to finish a book before I left for Darlene's. My stomach was hurting, but I didn't say anything about it. I didn't want my mother to keep me from sleeping at Darlene's.

I was only half-dressed. I had put on my shirt, but was still wearing just underpants on the bottom. I felt a wetness in my pants, but didn't pay any attention to it. I was too busy with my book.

My mother walked by my bed and stopped. I didn't pay any attention to her either.

"Linda," she said. No answer. "Linda!"

"What is it, Ma?" I looked up, annoyed.

"Come into the bathroom for a minute."

"What for?"

"Just come on in. Your underwear is dirty."

"What?" I sat up and looked at my pants. There was a small reddish stain spreading there. Suddenly, I was afraid.

"What is it, Ma? What's happening to me?"

"It's nothing to be afraid of. You've gotten your first period."

"My period? Oh no! I'm too young to have my period! I'll die if anyone finds out! Oh-h! Now I won't be able to sleep over at Darlene's. My whole vacation is ruined!" I felt tears stinging my eyes. I didn't know what to do.

"Calm down, Linda. Every girl gets her period sooner or later. Yours is just a little sooner than most. And you're not even that young. After all, you'll be twelve soon. As for going to Darlene's, there's no reason why you can't go. I'll show you how to wear a sanitary napkin. You can take some along with you. Just change them when you need to."

"Are you sure I'll be able to manage OK?"

"Of course." My mother got a box of sanitary napkins out of her closet. She showed me how to fasten one to my underpants so it wouldn't slip. I felt much better.

I couldn't decide whether or not to tell Darlene about getting my period. Part of me was proud of being grown up, but most of me was ashamed of it. I didn't know why I felt that way, especially with Darlene. But I did.

At twelve o'clock, we watched TV. Times Square was filled with thousands of people. They were there to watch the ball come down that would mark the start of the new year.

Everyone hugged and kissed each other. They shouted, "Happy New Year!" We could hear the horns blowing from the party next door and from the street below.

We looked out Darlene's window at the people in the streets. They were waving streamers and tooting on horns. Everyone seemed so happy on New Year's Eve.

I had expected to feel happy too. After all, this was the first time I had stayed up for New Year's. But I wasn't. Instead I felt a horrible emptiness inside. My stomach ached.

I sat down on Darlene's bed. Tears suddenly welled up in my eyes.

Darlene turned from the window in surprise. "What's the matter, Linda? Why are you crying?"

"I don't know," I sobbed. "All of a sudden I just felt awful!"

Darlene sat down next to me on the bed. She put her hand on my shoulder. "Hey, It's New Year's Eve. Everyone's supposed to be happy on New Year's Eve. Come on, Linda. Maybe if you talk about it you'll feel better."

"Oh, Darlene. I don't think I can, really."

"Come on, Linda. I tell you everything. We're best friends."

I guess I really did want to tell her, anyhow. If there was anyone who could understand how I felt now, it had to be Darlene. So, sniffling back my tears, I told her about getting my period.

"Oh, so that's it!" Darlene smiled at me, but she had tears in her eyes, too. "You know, I remember how awful I felt when I got my first period."

"You did?"

"Yes. I had the most violent fight with my mother that day. I guess in some strange way I must have blamed her because I developed so young. But she was pretty good about understanding." Darlene offered me a box of tissues.

I took one. "I guess my mother was good about understanding, too. She helped me a lot." I blew my nose. "And do you know what, Darlene. In one way, I'm a lot luckier than you were."

"What do you mean?"

I smiled. "It's a lot easier for me because I've got you to talk to. Having a friend has got to be one of the most important things in the world!"

"Even more important than having Jeff?" Darlene smiled teasingly.

"Now, Darlene," I laughed. "You know no self-respecting WHEBB club member could ever admit something like that!"

Darlene handed me another tissue. "Happy New Year, Linda!"

"Happy New Year, Darlene!" And now I really did feel happy.

Chapter Eight

As it got closer to the end of January, I was aware that Jeff's birthday was approaching. I really wanted to make up with him before his birthday, but I wasn't sure of how to do it.

Then one day, when we were lining up for assembly, Sue-Ann sneaked over to me and whispered, "Guess what? Jeff is having a birthday party next week. I'm invited!" She stuck her nose up in the air and marched smugly to her place in line.

I was crushed! To think that Jeff was inviting Sue-Ann to his party and not me! I still had a week, though. There had to be a way I could get him to invite me by then.

A light snow fell the next day. There was just

enough snow to stick to the cars parked on the street. This was the opportunity I had been waiting for.

On the way home from school, I hid behind a big station wagon. I rolled a batch of snowballs and stacked them in a pile. Then I waited for Jeff to pass by.

Soon my patience was rewarded. I spotted Jeff walking up the block. He was alone. I ducked down so he wouldn't see me. As soon as he passed by, I took careful aim. I reared back and threw the snowball right in the middle of his head. Smack! It splattered all over!

He whirled around to see who had hit him. For a moment, I worried about what his reaction would be when he saw it was me. His broad grin told me that I didn't have to.

"Why, you! Just wait till I get you back!" He raced for the nearest car to grab hold of some snow.

"Why should I wait? I'm ready right now!" I bombarded him with the rest of the snowballs. Then I ran!

He chased after me, one fist full of snow. I kept ahead of him until I slipped on an icy spot. He cornered me against a car. Then he presented me with his snow, right in the face!

"Hey! That's not fair! I didn't hit you in the face." I protested. I wiped myself off with my scarf.

"You poor little innocent thing," he answered. "That's exactly what you deserve. Now we're even. I'll even let you come to my party if you can behave yourself till then!"

"Party? What party?" Little did he know how long I'd waited for that moment.

"It's my birthday next week. I'm having a dancing party on Saturday."

"Yeah? Well who's coming?" I was playing it cool.

"Some of the kids from my class. You know, Sue-Ann and some of her friends. I also invited some kids from camp from last summer. Which reminds me—" He brushed off the snow from his jacket. "These kids from camp are a nice bunch. Do you think you can act like a lady for a change? Not like some monkey in a tree?"

He grinned when he said that, but I didn't know if he was kidding or not. I was really embarrassed by what he said. And then I began feeling angry. "That's a lousy, rotten thing for you to say to me, Jeff Davidson. Who do you think you are, anyway, Mr. Perfection? I can act as ladylike as anyone else when I want to. I just don't want to around you!"

"There you go again, shooting off your big mouth! That's exactly what I mean, Linda. I never know what kind of embarrassing thing you might say next!"

Now I was really angry. "Well, I certainly

wouldn't want to chance embarrassing you, Jeff. Just keep your dumb old party and your high-class friends from camp!"

I whirled around and stalked off down my block. Tears rolled down my face. I'd show him he couldn't speak to me like that! Imagine, calling me a monkey in a tree! Saying I didn't know how to act! He'd be the one to lose out by not having me at his party, not me!

The day of Jeff's party found me staring out the window. All my plans had amounted to nothing. I knew he wasn't going to miss me at the party. He was probably having a great time. It was I who was all alone and suffering.

I saw Sue-Ann passing across the street. She was carrying a gaily-wrapped package under her arm. Her birthday present for Jeff. Quickly, I ducked behind the drapes so she wouldn't see me. Just when I thought I had gotten away unseen, she turned and stuck her tongue out in my direction. Then she walked on, swinging and swaying toward Jeff's house.

I was too miserable to be mad at this point. I could picture Jeff, opening the door to greet Sue-Ann. She would walk in and give him her present. He would like it so much he would kiss her before she even got her coat off. All the "nice kids from camp" would cheer as he introduced her as his girlfriend.

I could have kicked myself! If only I had said the right thing, I could have been there at the party. Once again I had been defeated by my big mouth!

When we came to school on Monday, we found a substitute teacher instead of Miss Delaney. This was the first time she had been absent all year.

The substitute, Miss Chester, was young. She had curly brown hair, a soft, friendly-looking face, and twinkling blue eyes that laughed easily. She was just the kind of teacher that I had always wanted to have instead of an old battle-ax like Miss Delaney.

Miss Chester gave us the assignments that Miss Delaney had left for us, but she didn't pressure us to finish. She allowed us to talk to our friends if we didn't make too much noise. The morning was so pleasant that I couldn't help wishing that Miss Delaney would never come back.

After lunch, we received an unexpected visit from Mr. Wohl. He walked slowly to the front of the room and then turned to face us. His face looked as gray as his suit.

"Boys and girls. I have something important

to tell you," he said in a voice that was uncharacteristically quiet. All eyes focused on him at once.

"As you see, Miss Delaney is absent today," he began. "She'll be absent all week, and Miss Chester will be here to substitute for her." At these words, the entire class began to cheer. A whole week without Miss Delaney! But Mr. Wohl stifled us with his booming voice.

"Quiet!" he roared. "I said this was important! I expect you to hear me out without acting like a bunch of animals!"

No one moved. Mr. Wohl looked around the room. "That's better," he said. "And now, I want you to know why Miss Delaney is not here. Last night, her sister, who lived with her, took sick and died suddenly."

Died! The word cut through me like a knife. I hadn't known many people who had died in my lifetime. I didn't like to even think of death.

And Miss Delaney's sister! The one she was always telling us about. Somehow I had never thought of Miss Delaney as being able to be hurt by anything. But she must have been hurt by the death of her sister. She must be feeling awful right now. Even if she didn't show it, Miss Delaney must have feelings like the rest of us. Suddenly, I felt very bad for Miss Delaney.

Mr. Wohl was finishing talking now. "Miss

Delaney left complete plans for all your work. Miss Chester will make sure that you follow them. I expect you to give her the same respect that you give Miss Delaney. I don't expect to have to come up here to talk to this class for the rest of the week!"

Mr. Wohl frowned, turned, and stalked out of the room. Our class sat there in silence.

Miss Chester got up. "I knew about this news this morning, boys and girls," she said in her quiet voice. "But Mr. Wohl asked me not to tell you until he did. I've been trying to think of something nice we could do for Miss Delaney. Are there any ideas?"

Everyone was silent. It was hard to think of doing something nice for Miss Delaney when we had spent so much time disliking her.

My mind raced. I thought about Miss Delaney and the assignments she had given us this year. Most of them had been hard, but they had really made us think. And some of them had been interesting. Just last week she had taken us to see a television station to learn how it worked. That had been fun. Working on the school newspaper had been fun, too.

It was then I realized I had been wrong about Miss Delaney. She was hard and strict, and liked to brag, but we learned a lot from her. She really was a good teacher after all.

And now she would be living all alone. She

would be so lonely. We had to do something to cheer her up. She was our teacher.

"I have an idea," I surprised myself by saying. I saw Lisa roll her eyes at Rena, but I ignored them. I wasn't going to shut up now, no matter what people like Lisa thought of me.

"I think we should all do something creative. We can write a poem, or a story, or draw a picture. It doesn't matter what it is as long as it shows Miss Delaney we think she's a good teacher. We can put it all together in a book for her. It would make Miss Delaney proud to see we can do something on our own."

I dropped my eyes to the floor. I knew the kids would think I was a traitor or something, but I still had to say what I did.

The silence grew louder. I raised my head to look at Miss Chester and found her smiling at me. "I think that's an excellent idea," she said. "What about the rest of the class?"

Good old Suzy stuck by me like a true friend. "I agree with Linda," she said. "I'd like to write a poem."

"And I'll draw a picture," Jan Zieglebaum volunteered.

Once Jan, who never said much of anything, spoke up, it broke the ice. Everyone seemed to have something they wanted to do for Miss Delaney.

We worked on the project the entire afternoon. It made us all feel closer to Miss Delaney. Putting the book together, I almost felt good about her!

Then at the end of the week, we got more bad news. Without Miss Delaney to run things, Mr. Wohl decided to call off the Valentine's dance. Leave it to Miss Delaney to ruin things without even being there!

Chapter Nine

Finally! A snow that amounted to more than a little pile of slush! Saturday night, the heavy gray sky hung low over the city, smelling of snow. The first white flurries fell through the blackness and clung together.

I woke up early Sunday and ran to the window. Sure enough! A two-foot white blanket covered the world. The ugly gray city had taken on a strange beauty.

The snowplows had not yet come through. Traffic was at a standstill. The streets were empty, the stores closed. Down the block, I could see one lone figure, black against the whiteness.

I had to get out there! I threw on layers of

clothing—sweaters, hat, scarf, jacket, boots, and mittens. I clumped my way down the stairs.

I opened the door and the cold air hit me. A few flurries still fell. The wind stung them against my face. I stuck out my tongue to try to catch them. They melted from the warmth of me.

I began to walk, each step an effort. In front of me was the pure whiteness. Behind me was the trail of footprints I had left. I fought my way down the middle of the street. I loved the crunch of each step!

When I got to the park, I stopped. I was breathless, taking in the beauty of the scene. The ball field we had played on was hidden under a white cover. The trees glistened, frosted with icing. I could shut out the buildings and make believe I was in the beautiful country.

I climbed to where I could look out over the Hudson River. I watched the blocks of ice pushing through the water. The cliffs of New Jersey jutted into the sky, proudly showing off their white coats.

By then, a snowplow had come through the streets. People were out with shovels, struggling to free their cars. It was late enough for me to call for Suzy.

I struggled to Suzy's house. Should I go

upstairs or should I call her through the window in the hope that Jeff might hear me? I decided to take the chance.

"Suzy!" I yelled to the sixth floor.

She stuck her head out the window. "Hi, Linda. Isn't this great?"

"It sure is. Why don't you come down?"

"I will. I just have to eat breakfast first."

"OK. I'll wait for you out here." Leave it to Suzy. She put food before everything else.

While waiting, I busied myself rolling a small ball of snow into a larger one. That was for a base for a snowman.

My eyes kept focusing on Jeff's window. I hoped for some sign from him. Nothing happened. I went back to my snowman.

I was patting the first ball into shape when I heard his voice. "Oh it's you, Linda. I didn't recognize you with all that on!" He was standing right behind me!

"What do you expect me to wear in the snow? An evening gown?"

We both laughed. It was as if we had never been mad.

"Are you making a snowman?" he asked.

"Yeah. I thought one would look cute here peeping into your window," I grinned.

"I'll help. It'll come out better that way, for sure."

By rolling together, we managed to get a

huge ball right under his window. Our shoulders bumped as we worked, and it felt great. Two smaller balls and we had a snowman as tall as I was.

"What should we use for the face?" I asked.

"I'll go inside and get something," he said with a grin.

He came out with a bag of Oreo cookies. We split them open and licked out the cream inside. We used the cookie part for the eyes, nose, mouth, and buttons for our snowman. It was the best snowman I had ever made.

We stood together, looking at it with pride. I didn't look at Jeff. I was afraid to break that great moment.

He spoke first, bending over and packing some snow in his hands. "This snow is great for snowmen, but it's even better for something else."

"What?"

"Snowballs!" He threw the snow right in my face!

"Why, you!" I sputtered, wiping the snow away. Snow hung from my eyebrows and lashes. It froze the tip of my nose.

Jeff was laughing so hard he didn't even see me coming. With a flying leap, I tackled him around his knees. Plop! He landed sprawled out in the snow.

I climbed on top of him and sat on his well-padded stomach. "I've been waiting to give you this for a long time, Jeff Davidson. It's too bad that I missed your birthday, but better late than never!"

He squirmed, kicked, and yelled, trying to get me off him. I still got in the twelve birthday smacks that I owed him and one for good luck. By the time I had finished spanking him, I was laughing so hard that he was able to push me over. Down I went into the cold, wet snow.

By the time Suzy came down, we were soaked through and freezing. We went into Jeff's hall to warm up. Under a window hissed a radiator, sending warm steam through the hallway. The metal radiator cover served as a window seat.

We sat there and peeled off our top layers of wet clothing. My gloves stuck to me as I pulled out one finger at a time. They stung with pain as the warmth returned to them.

As I took off each boot, clumps of snow sloshed to the floor. A large wet puddle spread out from where I stood.

"Look what you've done to me!" I wailed.

"Done to you? Look what you've done to me!"

I looked. His hair was sopping and plastered down on his head. His shirt hung out from his sweater, and his big toe peeked from a hole in his right sock.

I began to laugh. "You've got to be the most ridiculous looking thing I've ever seen!"

"You wouldn't win any beauty contest yourself, Linda Berman!" And he laughed too.

I was cold and wet and scraggly. My fingers and toes hurt. But I never felt better in my life! Perhaps there was some hope for my WHEBB goals after all.

Chapter Ten

I had hoped that Miss Delaney would have changed when she returned to school after her sister's death. No such luck. She worked us harder than ever.

One day she decided that it was too much trouble for her to stand in line and buy herself subway tokens. She added *token-buyer* to our list of class jobs. Then she asked for a volunteer.

"Who would like to be my token-buyer?" she asked, carefully tucking her blouse into her skirt as usual. "The person has to be responsible. He or she would have the satisfaction of knowing my valuable time was being saved."

Her valuable time! Miss Delaney always

thought her time was more important than ours. Who would be dumb enough to volunteer for a job like token-buyer?

The room was silent. Everyone must have felt as I did. No one volunteered.

Suddenly I thought of the report cards that were due soon. It might help if Miss Delaney was feeling good about me when she was filling out my report card. It probably wouldn't be very much trouble to stop and buy her tokens. It was on my way home anyway.

I raised my hand. "I'll do it, Miss Delaney."

She beamed. "Well, Linda. Somehow I didn't expect you to volunteer. But I'm glad you did."

So every Thursday my friends would wait while I ran down to the token booth. I would hand the man Miss Delaney's money, buy the week's tokens, and slip them into her little token holder. I would put the holder in my pocket until I came back from lunch. Then I would place the holder on Miss Delaney's desk.

"Token-buying, traitor," Lisa Finklestein whispered to me as I passed her desk.

That hurt. I always hated kids who played up to teachers, and now I was being one. I tried to ignore Lisa's words.

For a while things went well. Miss Delaney seemed to have a better opinion of me. The kids stopped making a big deal about my playing up to her and buying the tokens.

Then came that awful Thursday in March. Darlene and Suzy waited for me to come out of the subway station with the tokens. As I walked up the steps, I heard a terrible howling sound in the tunnel behind me. My heart beat faster when I saw it was Jeff, Harley, Ken, and Marvin. They were hooting like a bunch of wild Indians.

"Ambush! Ambush!" Ken called, coming up behind me.

Then, before I knew what was happening, Jeff grabbed the tokens from my hand. He ran up the steps and took off.

"Hey! Give those back to me right now!" I ran after him as fast as I could.

Jeff turned around. "Sure Linda. I was just kidding." He walked toward me with the tokens in his hand.

Just as I was about to take them, he grinned. He tossed the tokens over my head and into the waiting hands of Ken.

I turned and ran after Ken. "Please, Ken," I begged. "Miss Delaney will kill me if anything happens to her tokens."

"You should have thought of that before you became token-buyer," he laughed, tossing the tokens to Harley.

"I think they'd look better down the sewer,

myself!" Harley stooped down and dangled them over the sewer grating.

"Harley!" I shrieked. "Don't you dare drop those tokens down the sewer! I'll tell Miss Delaney just what you're doing!"

"Okay, token-buyer, here's your precious tokens." Harley tossed them to me.

I missed and the holder went bouncing down the street. I ran after it and stuffed it into my jacket pocket. I ran the rest of the way home with cries of, "Token-buyer, token-buyer," ringing in my ears.

After lunch, I made it back to class without any further trouble. I stuck my tongue out at Harley as I passed his desk. I marched to the front of the room and reached into my jacket pocket for the tokens. My heart sank. There was nothing in my pocket at all!

"Well?" Miss Delaney stared at me. "Where are my tokens?"

"Just a moment, Miss Delaney." I searched my other pocket nervously. "They must be here somewhere." I fumbled through my skirt and blouse pockets hopelessly. I knew the tokens would not be there.

"Well?" Miss Delaney repeated. Her usual frown grew deeper between her eyes.

"I—uh—I can't seem to find them, Miss Delaney!"

"What do you mean, you can't find them?" she roared. "Don't you know I need those tokens to go home with today?"

"Y-yes, Miss Delaney," I mumbled, still looking through my pockets. "I can't imagine what could have happened to them. Unless— oh no, the boys!" I clapped my hand to my mouth in horror.

The eyes of the entire class were fixed upon me. Everyone seemed to sense that there was going to be big action.

"Boys? What boys? Did some boys take my tokens?" Miss Delaney rose from her seat. She was so tall!

"Well, er—yes. That is, no. I mean, uh— maybe!"

"What kind of answer is that?" She smashed her fist down on her desk. "Do you mean yes or do you mean no?"

I didn't know what to say. I didn't want to get the boys in trouble, too. I was pretty sure, however, that I had lost the tokens while they were chasing me home. I was never able to lie very well.

"Well, they didn't really take them. I mean, they did, but they gave them back."

"I don't know what you're talking about, young lady! You'd better tell me exactly what happened if you know what's good for you!"

Tears burned my eyes. Sobs built up in my throat. I was horrified. What if I started crying in front of the whole class?

Miss Delaney showed no mercy. She pulled the whole story out of me, bit by bit. With each word, her face grew redder. With each word, it was harder for me to hold back my tears.

"So!" she bellowed. "After I trusted you to buy my tokens, you went ahead and lost them. And why did you lose them? Because you were fooling around with boys instead of acting like a lady!"

Miss Delaney stopped to take a breath. Her voice grew unnaturally quiet. "When I allow a child to do a job, it is an honor. It shows that I think that child is responsible enough to do the job right. When a child disappoints me, it casts a shadow on my judgment. Then I become angry. Do you understand me, Linda Berman?"

Now her voice rose to a high shrill pitch. I shivered.

"Y-yes, Miss Delaney," I sobbed.

"Say it louder! I can't hear you!"

"Yes, Miss Delaney."

"That's more like it! And now, I want you to give me the name of every boy who was there this afternoon."

The last thing I wanted to do was tattle on

the boys. They would hate me forever. I said nothing.

"Well? Speak up, I say!"

I still said nothing. Tears began spilling from my eyes.

Miss Delaney towered over me. I could feel her breathing on my head. "Don't you play these little games with me, Linda Berman! I intend to find out exactly what happened, so you might as well tell me now. I'll have you standing up here all day if necessary!"

What could I do? There was no way to win with Miss Delaney. Painfully, I named Harley, Ken, and Marvin. But it was when I named Jeff that she really flipped out.

"So! We even have boys from other classes coming to lose my tokens!" She rocked back on her heels with rage. "Steven Warshinsky! Go to Mrs. Birnbaum's room and ask her to send Jeff Davidson to me right away!"

I thought I would die when Jeff walked into the room. There I was with tears streaming down my face. My nose was red and swollen. I stood there in shame.

Miss Delaney spent the entire afternoon yelling at each of us in turn. It was awful!

Before she finished, she made us all promise to chip in the money to buy her new tokens and a holder. She wanted it by the next afternoon at the latest. If she didn't have a new set by then, she would call all our mothers. And it was all because of me!

I didn't know what to tell my mother when I got home. I would have to ask her to lend me some money. I didn't have enough to pay for my share of the tokens.

"Ma," I began. "Something awful happened today with the tokens."

"I'll bet it did," she answered. "Look what I found under the desk!"

She held out her hand. There was the token holder. Every token was still in place.

I stood there with my mouth open. "Oh, no! It must have fallen out of my pocket when I took my jacket off at lunchtime!"

After all that had happened! Now what would everyone say when they found out the loss of the tokens had been all my fault? The boys had had nothing to do with it after all. I had gotten them into trouble for nothing. Would they ever speak to me again?

I didn't sleep all night. All I could think of was tokens, the boys, and Miss Delaney. I could just see the boys' reactions when I told them they had been blamed for nothing!

I was wrong about the boys. They all took the news like good sports. They were just glad not to have to pay for the tokens.

I wasn't wrong about Miss Delaney. Any other person would have been glad to get the tokens back. Not Miss Delaney. She just took the opportunity to yell at me some more.

I didn't want to go back to school after lunch. My mother convinced me I had to go. After all, there were still three months left in the school year. I couldn't stay home every day.

I walked into the classroom fearfully. I was prepared for more yelling. I didn't know how much more I could stand.

When we were all in our seats, Miss Delaney stood up and cleared her throat. "Boys and girls. May I have your attention?" All eyes focused on her.

"Linda Berman. Will you come to the front of the room?"

Not again! Slowly, I stood up and pushed in my chair. Sadly, I shuffled to the front of the room.

"Jan Zieglebaum. Will you come up here, too?"

Jan Zieglebaum! Why was she called up? She wasn't even there when the tokens were lost.

Miss Delaney stuck out her long neck. "Boys and girls," she announced. "Once again I am the only teacher who can proudly say she has students who passed the Huntington test.

This year two students have passed. Here they are, Jan Zieglebaum and Linda Berman!"

Passed the Huntington test? Me? For a moment, I was stunned. Then I felt myself swell with pride. I had made Huntington. Me. Not all the other girls who had gone to take the test that day. Not beautiful Lisa. Not old shapely-legs Rena. Me. And Jan. Only Jan and I would be able to go to that special school with all those bright and classy girls.

But then I felt a sinking feeling in my stomach. Girls. That was just the trouble. There were nothing but girls at Huntington. All my friends would be going together to the neighborhood junior high, 515. They would be having fun with the boys. No matter how good a school Huntington was, how could I go there without boys?

I ran all the way home from school that afternoon and up the stairs, two at a time. I couldn't wait to tell my mother the news.

"Ma!" I called, bursting in the door.

My mother came out of the kitchen, worriedly wiping her hands on her apron. "What's the matter, Linda? Did you have more trouble over the tokens?"

"No, Ma. That was this morning. You'll never guess what I found out this afternoon!"

"What is it?"

"I made Huntington, Ma! Jan Zieglebaum and I were the only girls in the whole school who made it!" Excitedly, I threw my books on my desk.

"Why, that's wonderful, Linda!" My mother's face lit up with pride. "Huntington is an excellent school. I'm so glad you'll be going there. It's an honor."

"The only problem is I'm not sure if I want to go there."

"Oh? Why wouldn't you?"

I sighed deeply. "Well, Ma, it's mostly that none of my friends, except Jan, will be going to Huntington. If I go there, I won't be part of our crowd anymore. And there are no boys in Huntington."

"That shouldn't matter, Linda. You can see your friends after school. Your education is what should come first. You want to be something when you grow up, don't you? If you graduate from a good school like Huntington, you can get into the best colleges. Going to Huntington would be the best thing you could do for your future."

"So you think I should go?"

"Yes, I think you should go," my mother said, very seriously. But then she put her arm around my shoulder and smiled at me. "But this is a decision you'll have to make for yourself, Linda. Talk to your father, your principal, and your teacher. That might help you make up your mind. You have the rest of the school year to decide."

Well, I talked to my father. Just as I figured, he thought I should go to Huntington for the education. So did Mr. Wohl. I didn't bother to talk to Miss Delaney again. I could tell she wanted me to go to Huntington by the way she acted when she told me I had passed the test. Every grown-up I spoke to seemed to think I should go to Huntington.

My friends were a different story. They all thought I should go to 515 with them.

It was a tough decision for me to make. Especially when I didn't even know what I wanted to be when I grew up. It scared me when I tried to think about it. There were so many possibilities—doing something I really enjoyed, like writing stories or painting, or doing something to help people, like being a doctor or a social worker.

Would going to Huntington really make a difference in my future? I just didn't know. How could I decide about my future when I was only in sixth grade?

June was three months away. I just hoped that something would happen by then to help me make up my mind.

Chapter Eleven

In April, my brothers came down with the chicken pox. The poor kids were sick during the nicest time of the year. For April brought the first warmth of spring. I unbuttoned my winter coat and joyfully breathed the spring-scented air.

Spring filled me with a new feeling of life. It also filled me with an even stronger desire to accomplish my WHEBB goals. For the time being, I put all thoughts of Huntington out of my mind.

A new baseball season began. We always knew where to find the boys now. The WHEBB club spent many hours sitting on the park wall or the schoolyard steps. We watched the boys play ball. We fooled around with them and each other. It was fun but something was missing. We wanted something more.

There was a new boy in Darlene's class. His name was Lawrence Carlson. He was tall and looked older than the other boys. He acted older, too. He liked Darlene, and he wasn't afraid to show it. The other boys could have used a lesson from Lawrence. They were still so immature.

Maybe it was Lawrence's influence that did it. One day, Ken passed out little pieces of folded construction paper in the schoolyard. He gave one to Darlene, one to Suzy, and one to me. I almost flipped when I opened mine and read:

In honor of Easter and Ken's birthday
You're invited to a party
Place: Ken's house—709 W 177 Street
Time: 3:45 on Wednesday—the last day of
    school

Unbelievable! The boys were actually giving a party! All of WHEBB was invited! After doing some detective work, we found out exactly who else was coming. Lisa and Rena were the other girls invited. We could have lived without them. But Ken, Harley, Jeff, Marvin, and Lawrence were the boys. And that, except for Marvin, was absolutely fantastic!

So Wednesday afternoon I ran home from school. Ten days of freedom and a party with the boys! It was almost too good to be true.

I went into the bathroom to change out of my school clothes. As I took off my blouse, I saw some strange-looking spots on my stomach. They itched and I scratched one without thinking.

Oh, no! It couldn't be—not the chicken pox! Not now right before Easter vacation! Not on the day of the party!

What was I going to do? If I told my mother, she never would let me go to the party. Besides, I wasn't sure that it really was chicken pox. Maybe it was just a rash.

I decided to go to the party. If I forgot about the marks on my stomach, maybe they would go away.

WHEBB had decided to meet on my corner and walk together to the party. I ran out as soon as I heard Suzy call me through my window. I was afraid that if my mother saw me, she would know that something was wrong. She has a sixth sense for things like that.

"Have a good time!" My mother called after me.

"Thanks, Ma!" I darted out the door.

When we got to the party, Ken's mother did her best to make us feel at home. She brought out the refreshments and made sure we ate plenty of pizza. And after we finished eating, she left us alone.

While we were busy with the food, everything was fine. We laughed and joked together, just like we did walking home from school each day. But once the pizza was finished and someone put on a record, everything seemed to change. We sat there awkwardly on Ken's sofa and living room chairs. It was as if we were strangers. Everyone was uncomfortable. No one knew how to act.

I had to do something. I waited until a fast dance was playing. "Come on, Darlene, let's dance," I said. Someone had to be first.

Once Darlene and I were up, Lisa and Rena got up and danced. Suzy went over to the snack table and began eating potato chips. Still none of the boys moved.

The next record was slow. I wasn't about to dance a slow dance with Darlene in front of all the boys.

We stood there, feeling silly. Then Lawrence came over to where we were standing.

"Let's dance, Darlene," he said with authority. Darlene didn't even have a chance to think.

Lawrence took her hand and led her to the middle of the room. He put his arm around her and began to dance.

They did look good together. Lawrence was the only boy there who was taller than Darlene. They looked so grown up, dancing like that.

I stood watching them and wishing I could dance that way with Jeff. Why were he and the other boys so immature? If I were a boy, I would ask me to dance for sure!

I closed my eyes, listened to the music, and pictured myself in Jeff's arms. We would whirl around softly, staring into each other's eyes. Jeff would bend over to kiss me tenderly.

"Hey, Berman! Did you come to this party to sleep or dance?"

My eyes flew open. There was Jeff with his hand stretched toward mine. I had just been asked to dance!

This was the moment I had been waiting for. Finally, my chance to be in Jeff's arms. But what if I had the chicken pox? I could give it to him!

"I'll be back in a minute, Jeff." I turned away from him and ran into the bathroom.

I sat on the toilet seat and pulled up my shirt. The few marks that had been there earlier had multiplied. My head was beginning to ache as well. Now there was no doubt left. I had the chicken pox.

I looked in the mirror to see if there were any signs on my face. A few pox had appeared behind my ears and on my neck. Some had crept over my right cheek. Surely everyone would notice!

What should I do? I sat on the sink, staring into the mirror. I felt very sick.

There was a sudden rapping on the bathroom door. "Linda! Are you still in there?" It was Darlene's voice.

I unlocked the door and let her in. "Oh, Darlene, it's you. Having a good time?" I tried to look cheerful.

"Fantastic!" she bubbled. "That Lawrence Carlson is something else—boy does he hold me tight when we dance! I just know Harley is getting jealous watching us. But what about you?"

"What do you mean, what about me?" I asked nervously.

"You've been in here for ages. It's not like you to pass up dancing with Jeff for sitting in the bathroom!"

"Ha-ha-very funny." I tried to smirk. But then I caught sight of my poxy face in the mirror. "Oh, no," I groaned.

"What is it, Linda?" Darlene looked worried.

Tearfully, I told Darlene everything. "What am I going to do now?" I wailed. "If I go out there, everyone will see the pox on my face."

Darlene examined me in the light. "Are you talking about those few little pink marks on your cheek? No one will even notice them if you don't say anything."

"But I'm contagious! What if I give someone the chicken pox? I would feel awful!"

"Well, Linda, the damage is already done. If anyone is going to get the chicken pox from you, they've already been exposed. Just come out and act like nothing is wrong. And make sure that you dance with Marvin Haven a lot." Darlene gave a little laugh. "He deserves to get the chicken pox!"

How I made it through the party I'll never know. When I got home, my head was splitting. I was running a fever too.

It was Easter vacation, and I had to stay in bed with one of the worst cases of chicken pox ever. I was miserable!

It was my third day in bed. I was covered with calamine lotion from head to foot. I itched so badly that I couldn't stop scratching. Life was pure torture.

I heard my father come home from work. He peered into the living room and smiled at me. "Here's something to keep you busy," he said, tossing a letter on my bed. "I found it under the door."

I picked up the envelope, my hands shaking. There, on the front, was written: For Linda Berman *only!*

The return address was:

> Jeff's Delivery Service
> 379 Ft. Washington Avenue
> New York

I opened it as carefully as I could. I wanted to save that envelope forever. I couldn't wait to see what was inside. My heart pounded as I read:

> I hear you're sick. That's too-oo bad. I had the chicken pox once before, so I guess I'm not going to catch it from you. See you in the schoolyard when you're better.
>
> > Your friend,
> > Jeff Davidson

I stared at the letter with disbelief. Imagine, Jeff writing me a nice note like that! Maybe he did like me after all. Maybe my WHEBB goals were finally going to get somewhere. Maybe—

I didn't want to get my hopes up too high. But why else would he bother to send me that note?

Chapter Twelve

The day we returned to school after Easter vacation was the day Jan Zieglebaum made her decision. She was going to go to Huntington instead of 515. Now the pressure was really on me to make up my mind.

Miss Delaney positively beamed when she heard Jan's news. Sure, I thought bitterly. Miss Delaney is glad that Jan's going to Huntington. It makes Miss Delaney look good when one of her students goes there. And what does she know about liking boys anyway?

I waited until Miss Delaney left the room. I got out of my seat and went over to Jan's table. I knew this was dangerous. One of Delaney's primary rules is that no one is to be out of his or her seat when she leaves the room. But I was just dying to speak to Jan about Huntington. And I figured I had enough time to get back to my seat before Miss Delaney returned.

"What made you decide to go to Huntington, Jan?" I whispered. The last time I had spoken to Jan about going, she was as undecided as I was. With Jan, the problem really wasn't that there were no boys at Huntington. Her mother was afraid to let her go that long distance on the bus.

"My mother decided for me," Jan admitted sheepishly. "She went over to look at 515 and didn't like it. Too many tough kids and all that. She figured I'm better off taking a long trip and being with nice girls than going to a school in our neighborhood with those other types."

"Oh," I said disappointedly. I was hoping that Jan would have said something that would help me make up my own mind. But the type of kids going to 515 didn't bother me at all. In fact, if Jan's mother didn't like them, I figured the chances were that I would.

"But, what if—" I began. I never had a chance to finish my question. Miss Delaney came back to the room and caught me out of my seat.

"Linda Berman!" she roared. "What are you doing out of your seat? You've been in my room long enough now to know the rules!"

111

I swallowed hard. "Yes, Miss Delaney," I managed to say. "I-I, uh, I just wanted to speak to Jan about Huntington."

"Well, it could have waited until school was out! A rule is a rule." Miss Delaney puffed up her chest with air and tucked in her blouse. "Suppose you just stay after school today, and we'll talk about it."

"Yes, Miss Delaney," I replied. Of all the rotten luck! I hadn't seen Jeff since the day of Ken's party. I had been counting on running into him on the way home from school. Now, all I had to look forward to was another scolding from Miss Delaney!

So at three o'clock, I remained in my seat as the rest of the class filed out to freedom. Miss Delaney sat at her desk and watched everyone leave. Then she turned and stared at me sternly.

"Well, Linda. What do you have to say for yourself?"

"I'm sorry, Miss Delaney," I began. "Huntington's been on my mind a lot recently. I can't seem to decide whether or not I want to go there. My parents, Mr. Wohl, and you seem to think I should go. My friends think I should go to 515 with them. I'm so confused. I thought maybe Jan could tell me something to help make up my mind."

Miss Delaney frowned deeply. "I'm surprised at you, Linda. An intelligent girl like you should know that there's nothing that Jan could tell you that should make up your mind. The reasons that make it right or wrong for Jan to go to Huntington are not the same reasons that make it right or wrong for you. This is something that you are going to have to decide by yourself. You have to do what's right for you, Linda, and not worry so much about what other people think."

I looked at Miss Delaney in surprise. "But, Miss Delaney. I thought you wanted me to go to Huntington!"

"I do. But that's speaking from a strictly educational viewpoint. There are not many schools finer than Huntington. But I realize that there are more things in life than just school. A bright girl like you will manage to become educated wherever you go. If your social life matters that much to you, you have to consider that aspect, too. I wish I had when I was younger!"

I stared at Miss Delaney, my eyes bulging with amazement. Could this be the same Miss Delaney who had been my teacher all year? The one who wore the accomplishments of her students like badges on her chest? Did I really hear her tell me my social life was as important to consider as my education? Did Miss Delaney actually believe that friends were important too? And BOYS?

I had thought that I had Miss Delaney all figured out. Suddenly I realized I had been unfair to her. I didn't understand her at all.

"Why don't you relax a bit about Huntington, Linda?" she asked, her voice surprisingly soft. "You have until the end of June to make up your mind. I'm sure that, by then, something will happen to help you decide."

"Yes, Miss Delaney," I said quietly. "I'll try."

"Good," she said, rising from her desk and tucking in her blouse. "You may go, now. Just keep in mind what I said."

"I will, Miss Delaney." I happily began gathering up my books.

"And, Linda." Her voice held me back.

"Yes, Miss Delaney?"

"I know I thanked the class as a group for that lovely book you made for me when my sister died. But Miss Chester told me that it was your idea and that it was you who put it together. I just wanted to tell you that I appreciated it very much."

My face burned with embarrassed pleasure. I didn't know what to say.

"Oh—uh. It was nothing, Miss Delaney. We all just wanted you to know that we think you're a great teacher—even if you are strict!"

I looked up at Miss Delaney's face, then. The most amazing thing happened. The frown lines that had seemed etched into her face changed. Miss Delaney's face actually crinkled up into a smile! At that moment I was really, truly, glad to have her as a teacher.

The next week our school newspaper ran an important notice. Tryouts were starting for our school operetta. This was the most important production of the year. The sixth grade would present the show as part of our graduation ceremony. All the parents and school board members would be invited.

I didn't have any false hopes of getting a good role. Since the show was an operetta, all the leads would have to sing. Unfortunately, when singing voices were handed out, I was last in line.

I could never hear it, myself, of course. In fact, I used to think I did a pretty good job singing. Then, in first grade, I noticed my teacher skipping over me when it was my turn to sing. That made me suspicious.

Sometimes I would sing for the pure joy of it. After years of having people ask me to stop, I caught on. I accept it. I just can't sing.

I did still hope that I would get a part in the chorus. I can act even though I can't sing. And the entire cast would be excused from classes for all the practices.

The tryouts were to be on Thursday. On Wednesday, I went home and practiced my singing all afternoon. I don't know if it was all that singing that strained my throat. By 7 o'clock that night my throat was sore. I could hardly swallow. By 8 o'clock my mother noticed that I was sick.

I was in the kitchen doing my homework. I kept sweating, even though it wasn't hot. My mother was finishing drying the supper dishes. She put down her dish towel and looked at me.

"Linda, are you OK?"

"Sure, Ma," my voice creaked. "Why?"

"Your face looks flushed to me. Do you have a fever?"

"Oh, no. Why would I have a fever?" A feeling of panic spread over me.

"Your face just looks too red. Come here. Let me feel your forehead." She touched her lips to my head. "Just as I thought. You have a temperature!"

"How could that be? I just got over being sick with the chicken pox," I moaned.

"You were probably in a run-down condition. That makes it easier to catch something else." My mother frowned. "Especially when you're always knocking yourself out running after boys!"

"Ma! I'm not always running after boys!"

"Well, in any case, you'll have to stay home from school tomorrow and rest."

"Tomorrow! Tomorrow's the tryouts for the operetta. I have to go to school tomorrow or I won't get a part," I pleaded.

"Then the operetta will just have to manage without you," my mother said firmly. "You can't go to school with a fever."

The next day, I was miserable. Why did I always have to get sick at the worst possible time? My throat was so sore I could hardly swallow. But that didn't hurt as much as missing out on the operetta.

I sat in bed watching the hands of the clock slowly move toward three. I was dying to know what had happened with the operetta.

Finally, it was three-fifteen. I raced to the phone and dialed Suzy's number.

"You'll never guess who got the lead role in the operetta!" Suzy announced. "Jeff Davidson, himself!"

"Jeff!" I repeated, stunned. "I didn't even know he could sing."

"Well, he can. Miss Delaney picked him right away."

I groaned. Jeff, the lead role in the play. Of all the rotten luck. My only chance to be in the same play with him, and I had to blow it by missing the tryouts.

Then I was struck by a horrible thought. "Suzy! The female lead—don't tell me Miss Delaney gave that to Sue-Ann Fein!"

"Nope!" Suzy replied with her customary giggle. "Sue-Ann got the second most important part, but not the lead. That was given to Lisa Finklestein."

"Lisa Finklestein! I should have known. Lovely Lisa is Miss Delaney's favorite." Sadly, I hung up the phone.

I climbed back into bed even though I no longer had a fever. How was I going to stand it for the rest of the year? Jeff in a play with both Sue-Ann and Lisa, and I was stuck in the classroom with the rejects from the tryouts. And all because of a sore throat!

When I got back to school on Monday, I felt awful. In the afternoon, Miss Delaney called all the kids who had made it into the operetta together for the first practice. I sat there, my head drooping on my hands. All my friends seemed to have gotten some sort of role. They were all getting up around me.

Then I heard Miss Delaney say my name. "Linda! I've decided you might make a good prompter for the play. So you may come with us to rehearsal."

I looked up at Miss Delaney and found her smiling at me. I couldn't believe it. Miss Delaney, actually going out of her way to be nice to me!

"Yes, Miss Delaney!" I bounded out of my seat. I didn't even know what a prompter was, but I didn't care.

It turned out that I sit in the front row holding the script of the play. In case anyone forgets his lines, I whisper them. That way, the cast can hear but the audience can't.

It wasn't as good as having the lead role, or even a good part like Sue-Ann's. But I got to go to rehearsals every day and see Jeff, and that was what really counted.

Chapter Thirteen

The school year was nearing an end. The WHEBB club decided it was time to get our autograph books. Darlene talked us into buying the most expensive model. It cost three weeks' allowance, but it was something I wanted to keep forever.

We all bought the same book, but in different colors. Darlene's was pink, Suzy's was yellow, and mine was white. Each page was in a different pastel color. There was a zipper around the whole book. In the back were pages for photographs.

We sat in my hallway and wrote in each other's books. It took me a long time to think of something special to write to Darlene and Suzy. After all, they were my best friends.

When I read what they had written in my book, I couldn't help laughing. Suzy wrote:

> *They grow lemons in Louisiana,*
> *They grow lemons in Florida too,*
> *But it takes a state like New York State*
> *To grow a nut like you!!!*
>
> > *Love, your (best?) friend, Suzy*

"Gee thanks, Suzy," I pretended to be hurt. "It really helps when your best friend thinks you're a nut!"

"I mean you're a *lovable* nut," she corrected with a giggle.

Darlene wrote:

> *Beware of boys with eyes of brown,*
> *They'll kiss you once and turn around.*
> *Beware of boys with eyes of blue,*
> *They'll kiss you once and ask for two!*
>
> > *Love, your (best?) friend,*
> > *Darlene*

"How do you know so much about kisses?" I asked Darlene.

"Oh, you'd be surprised," she answered, a strange look on her face.

Ordinarily, I would have questioned Darlene about that statement, but now I was too anxious to get my autograph book signed by Jeff. I zipped the book shut and fingered the gold lettering that said, AUTOGRAPHS. "Let's go to the ball field," I said. "I can't wait to get Jeff to sign my sixteenth page."

"Do you think he knows what that means?" asked Suzy.

"How could he not know?" Darlene answered. "Everyone knows the sixteenth page is for the one you love. Unless they're living in the dark ages."

"Isn't that where Jeff is living?" Suzy giggled.

"Hey, watch it," I said. "We'll see which WHEBB member can get her special boy to sign her sixteenth page first. I'll bet you that I'll be the one. Jeff is sure to sign it for me."

"We'll see," said Darlene. And we all started off for the park.

As we got closer to the ball field, I started losing my confidence. It was pretty dumb of me to bet on Jeff that way when I never knew how he was going to act. He was so changeable. One day, he acted like he really liked me. The next day, he paid no attention to me at all. What if this was a bad day? What if Jeff refused to sign my sixteenth page in front of everyone?

I grasped my autograph book and pen tightly as we approached the park wall. We could hear them shouting before we could see them. The boys, including Jeff, were all there playing ball.

"How are we going to do this?" Suzy giggled nervously.

Darlene boosted herself up on the wall. She swung her legs around and let them dangle. "The game will be over soon. The boys will come up here when they see us. We'll just wait." She threw her hair back over her shoulder. She looked very sexy.

"Hi, Darlene!" Lawrence Carlson called up to her. "You'd better be careful or you'll fall right into my arms!"

"I'm sure you'll catch me then," Darlene blinked her eyes and stayed right where she was.

"Is that your autograph book you're holding?" Lawrence came closer.

"Sure is. Come up here and you can sign it. You'll be the first boy in my book." Darlene arched her back. Her tee shirt clung to her. Lawrence could hardly take his eyes away. With a running jump, he pulled himself up next to her.

He looked into her eyes and smiled his slow smile. "Does that mean I'm your number one? I'll sign your sixteenth page."

Darlene blushed as red as her hair. "Well, OK!"

Lawrence took the pen from her hand. He carefully counted sixteen pages and began to write. Darlene's eyes were fixed on Lawrence. I looked at Suzy over his head and shrugged. What was the matter with Darlene? I couldn't believe that she was letting Lawrence sign her sixteenth page instead of Harley!

A cheer went up from below. The game had ended. The boys began climbing up the wall. They were in a good mood, for their team, the Royals, had won. This was a new team that had been started by one of the men in the neighborhood. They played ball on Saturdays against other neighborhood teams.

Autograph books were being pulled out from all sides. Everyone began signing everyone else's. I could hardly keep track of mine.

Rena and Lisa came over with their autograph books. And down the block, I could see Sue-Ann Fein coming with hers!

My thoughts raced. I didn't want Jeff to sign my book in the middle of a crowd like this. I had to think of some way to get him away from the others before Sue-Ann got there!

I grabbed my book away from Marvin Haven before he could finish what he was writing. He looked shocked, but I didn't care.

"See you later!" I called to Darlene and Suzy.

I jumped down from the wall as easily as any boy. I ran through the bushes to where Jeff was gathering his things together. He had just picked up his bat and was reaching for his glove. I scooted by him and grabbed the glove.

"Gee, look at this neat glove I found!" I called. I ran across the ball field toward the back of the park. I sure hoped he would follow me.

"Hey, Berman, give that back! That's my good glove!"

"You want it? Come and get it!" I kept on running.

Jeff finally took off after me. I headed for the terrace way in the back of the park. It overlooked the Hudson River. I sped up the steps of the terrace.

Out of breath, I slowed down a little. Jeff caught up to me. He grabbed me around the waist and pulled me down on a bench.

"OK, Berman. Let's have the glove!" He squeezed me tighter.

I wouldn't let go. "You can have your glove," I smiled. "When you sign my autograph book!"

"Oh! So that's your game!" His eyes twinkled. "Well, if that's the only way I'll get my glove back, hand it over!"

I gave him his glove and my book. I was thrilled to see him start counting the pages. He was going to sign my sixteenth page! And I hadn't even asked him!

"Hey, what's this?" He looked at me. "Marvin Haven already signed your sixteenth page!"

"What?" I grabbed the book back from him and counted for myself. "Why that dirty creep! He must have done that on purpose! My whole autograph book is ruined! What will the WHEBB club say when they find out that Marvin Haven signed my sixteenth page?" In anger, I kicked the bench.

Jeff laughed. "Calm down, Linda. Why don't you think instead of storming around like that? All we have to do is tape my page in front of Marvin's. Then I'll be on the sixteenth page. No one will know the difference."

I stopped kicking and smiled. "Great idea, Jeff! Why didn't I think of that?" I sat down next to him, looking around at the scenery so I wouldn't have to watch him write.

I gazed at the Hudson River and the lazy way it flowed under the George Washington Bridge. The sun glinted off the bridge and made me blink. I took a deep breath and focused on Jeff once again. What would he write in my book?

"Here you go." He handed the book to me.

I could feel my heart beating as I began to read:

The door is locked; the key is in the cellar.
There's no one home but Linda and her feller.
  (Jeff)
Seriously, I hope this graduation is the
  foundation of
your education, whether you go on to
  Huntington or 515.

> *Your boyfriend,*
> *Jeff Davidson*

I held the book tightly. I ran my fingers over the ink. I couldn't believe that Jeff could write something so nice. And he actually signed it, "your boyfriend"!

Of course, it did bring my mind back to what I had been trying to block out. Was I going to Huntington or to 515 next year? I pushed thoughts of Huntington away once again. Going to Huntington meant not being with Jeff. It meant not being with boys at all. I didn't want to think about that now. I wanted to think about Jeff and how much I liked him.

I took a deep breath, trying to think of something to say to him. My heart was pounding so!

Suddenly I heard loud giggling and catcalls and a shrill voice shattered the wonderful mood. "Look at the two lovers!"

I turned around and saw that the whole crowd of kids from the wall were marching up the terrace steps. They had come in search of us. In the lead was Sue-Ann Fein!

Sue-Ann marched over to our bench. She paid no attention to me, but sat down on the other side of Jeff. She batted her eyelashes at him sexily. Then she plopped her autograph book in his lap and smiled. "I've saved my sixteenth page for you, Jeff!"

I waited for him to say no. He didn't. He smiled sheepishly. Without even looking at me, he began writing in her book. In front of everyone! I could have died!

I couldn't stand it! I took my book and stormed off the terrace. Darn that Jeff! When was he going to make up his mind!

I ran down the terrace steps and around the back of the park. I sat down on the wall overlooking the Hudson River. Tears burned my eyes. No one was there, so I just let the tears fall.

"Hey, Linda. What's the matter?"

I looked around hopefully. It was only Darlene.

"Oh, Darlene," I sobbed. "I just can't stand it! One moment everything is going great with Jeff. The next moment something happens to ruin it!"

Darlene swung up on the wall next to me. "Tell me what happened, Linda."

"Well," I sniffled. "Jeff finally signed my sixteenth page. He wrote something really sweet, and he even signed it, "your boyfriend." Then that Sue-Ann came along. She asked him to sign her sixteenth page, and he forgets I exist!" I sobbed aloud.

"Careful!" Darlene handed me a crumpled tissue from her pocket. "You're getting your autograph book all full of tears. But I know just how you feel, Linda. I'm confused half the time, myself. One minute I'm nuts about Harley. Then he ignores me and I feel awful. Then Lawrence pays me attention and I think I might really like him." As she said this, tears came to her eyes, too.

I stopped my crying and I looked at her. "Is that why you let Lawrence sign your sixteenth page instead of Harley?"

Now Darlene was sniffling worse than I was. "Yeah. Harley is such a child. Lawrence acts like a man. Do you know that he wrote a story? It was about what it's like for a boy to suddenly start liking girls. He made me realize that boys really do have the same feelings that we do. Remember how, when we first started the WHEBB club, we weren't sure? But try as I do, I still can't get Harley out of my mind. Why can't he grow up already?"

Chapter Fourteen

The arrival of June meant graduation was approaching fast. I still hadn't made up my mind about Huntington. I was tired of talking about it, tired of thinking about it. I just hoped that when the time came, I would make the right decision.

In honor of graduation, my mother decided I could have a new dress. I hate to shop, but I really wanted a new dress. The operetta was coming up, and after that Lawrence was having a party. I had to look my best for that. Everyone from our crowd was invited. This was the last party of the school year. My last chance to win out with Jeff over Sue-Ann Fein.

So Saturday found us fighting the crowds at Alexander's department store. My mother ignored my protests and took me to the children's department. She picked out three dresses in size fourteen for me to try on. My mother thought they were *adorable*. I thought they were for babies.

I tried on the first dress. It was too tight across the chest. So were the other two. I must have done some growing since the last time I shopped.

My mother looked at me and sighed. "I guess we'll have to try the junior department."

I smiled. The junior department was where I had wanted to go in the first place.

There I found the perfect dress. It was light blue, which brought out the blue of my eyes. It fitted closely around my waist. In it I looked like I had a real figure.

My mother noticed that, too. "If you want to wear that dress, Linda, you're going to have to get a bra."

A bra! I looked at myself in the mirror again. My mother was right. I couldn't hide it in a dress like this one. I was getting breasts!

"Okay, Ma. I'll get a bra, but only to wear with this dress. I don't need it for every day."

"You will before too long," my mother said. "We'll get you one of those teen bras. The kind that grow with you."

We paid for the dress. Then we went to the underwear department. There was an old lady working at the bra counter. She must have been a little deaf. She made my mother repeat herself. Twice. And each time louder.

"My daughter needs her first bra. A Bra! She needs a BRA!"

The old lady's head bobbed up and down. "Oh, a FIRST BRA!" she yelled. "How sweet! Here are two good ones to try."

There happened to be a sale on girdles that day. The underwear department was full of bargain-hunting ladies. Every one of them stopped searching through the pile of girdles so they could see whether or not I needed a bra. I folded my arms over my chest and followed my mother into the dressing room.

I tried on both bras. It was a struggle to get into them. What a pain to be grown up! Finally my mother showed me a trick way to fasten a bra. You put the back part in the front. You hooked it up. Then you twisted it around the right way and slipped it over your shoulders. It was on!

I looked at myself in the mirror. It was so strange to see myself in a bra. I wasn't sure I liked it. I tried my new dress on over it. It did look better with a bra.

I turned around so I could see my back in the mirror. There was a telltale bulge across my back. Anyone who looked could tell I was wearing a bra.

I sighed. What could I do? Maybe if I got lucky no one at the party would notice that I, Linda Berman, was wearing a bra!

The day of the operetta was a busy one. During final practice the kids had made lots of mistakes. I felt really important being prompter. I was needed.

The auditorium was filled with kids and parents. You could feel the excitement in the air. Everyone was nervous. Everyone was afraid he'd forget his lines. I went around reassuring everyone.

"Don't worry, I'll be sitting right in the first row." I told Jeff. He looked so adorable in his costume. He was wearing embroidered Swiss shorts and knee socks. I could see the muscles in his legs.

Sue-Ann Fein pushed between us. "Come on Jeff, let's practice before curtain time." She led him away by the arm. Darn her! I just wished she'd forget her lines. There was no way that I would prompt her!

I didn't get my revenge. Sue-Ann remembered every line. So did everyone else. I didn't get a chance to prompt anyone at all!

My mother came to school to see the operetta. Afterwards, she stayed to talk to Mr.

Wohl. He called me down to his office. I knew what it was about. Time had run out. I had to make my decision about going to Huntington or 515.

Mr. Wohl sat behind his huge wooden desk. He towered over it. "Sit down, Linda," he boomed. He pointed to an empty seat in front of him. My mother sat to one side of the desk. I felt very small sitting there.

"Your mother and I have been talking about whether or not you're going to Huntington. Jan Zeiglebaum is all set to go. You've waited until the very last day to answer. We have to know your decision now. There's a lot of paperwork that has to be done by the end of the year. So what have you decided?"

Mr. Wohl finished speaking and sat back in his chair. My mother looked at me hopefully. She didn't say anything, but I knew how she felt.

I really didn't know what to do. I had blocked all thoughts of Huntington out of my mind. I had been so busy with school, the weekly "What's Happening," the WHEBB club, and boys! It had been easy not to think of Huntington. Now I had to decide.

My mind raced. I thought of my crowd. They would be meeting at my corner candy store to walk together to 515 every day. If I went to Huntington, I would be left out. The only one I would have to ride with on that long bus trip was Jan.

But then, maybe I would make new friends. Maybe they would be even more interesting than the ones I had now. After all, the brightest girls from the whole city came to Huntington.

Girls! That was just the problem! How could I sit each day in a classroom with no boys? When would I see Jeff? Would I still be invited to my crowd's parties?

"Boys—you shouldn't be thinking of boys," my father's words rang in my head. "You should be thinking of your education."

My father was always telling me that the boys who seemed so important to me now wouldn't in a year or two. Crowds always break up. The friends who are so close now drift apart. Could that be true?

My friends were almost a part of me. They would stick with me even if I went to Huntington. Or would they?

I thought of my father again. He and my mother both came to America mostly for the education. They both struggled to finish high school. They went at night. During the day they worked to help support their families. No wonder education was so important to them!

"OK, I'll go to Huntington!" It wasn't until I heard the words that I knew I really had said them. I didn't know why I had decided to go. I didn't know if it was the right decision. But once I had made up my mind, I felt a lot lighter.

Mr. Wohl beamed. My mother's face lit up with a smile. They, at least, thought I did the right thing.

But my friends were not so sure.

"You're breaking up the WHEBB club," Darlene accused. We were walking together to Lawrence's party. "How could you do that? How can you subject yourself to day after day with no boys?"

"Everyone at Huntington is probably just like Jan," giggled Suzy. "Imagine, thirty Jan Zieglebaum's in one room!"

"Let's forget about Huntington," I pleaded. "I decided, and it's too late to change now. Let's talk about the party. Do you think Lawrence will have kissing games?"

"Knowing Lawrence, there will be plenty of kissing games." Suzy covered her mouth with glee. "He can't wait to have an excuse to kiss Darlene!"

"He doesn't need an excuse," Darlene said, shaking back her hair. The rays of the setting sun reflected off it, shining like fire. "He's already kissed me!"

Suzy and I stopped short. We both began to question Darlene at once. "Where? When? Why? How? What did it feel like? Was it on the lips? Was he a good kisser? Did you close your eyes? Did you know what to do? Did you act hard to get?"

"Hold it, hold it!" Darlene took a step backwards. "If you stop asking questions, I'll tell you what happened!"

"Go ahead. Tell us!" I urged. "But let's keep walking. I don't want to be late for the party."

"Well, Lawrence and I were sitting on the wall by the river this afternoon. It was at our 'cry spot,' Linda."

Our "cry spot"! Darlene took Lawrence to our secret "cry spot"! The traitor! I gave her a dirty look.

She didn't even notice. "I was feeling really sad about things—you know, school's ending and everyone's going away for the summer."

We nodded approval.

"I started crying. Before I knew it, he had his arm around me to comfort me. It seemed so natural for him to bend over and kiss me. I kissed him right back! I didn't even think of whether I had to keep my eyes closed or my lips open. I guess I'm just a natural kisser! And Lawrence really knows how to kiss!"

"Wow!" Suzy breathed.

"What about Harley?" I asked.

"Harley? Oh, I still think he's the cutest. He just has some growing up to do. I'll be happy to kiss him at the party too. I can't wait for the kissing games to start!"

Lawrence's party was the biggest of the whole school year. Everyone was there. Everyone was all dressed up. The boys wore jackets and ties. The girls wore their graduation dresses.

I felt good about myself in my new dress. I was just a little nervous, not wanting anyone to notice my new bra. Sure enough, Rena Widmark came over and ran her shapely fingers up my back!

"I see you're wearing a bra, Linda!" She raised her voice so everyone could hear her. She grabbed my bra strap from the back. She stretched it and let it go. It made a snapping noise.

"Ping! Robin Hood! Snap your bow!" She laughed.

I could have punched her in the teeth. Everyone in the room was laughing. Everyone knew that I was wearing a bra! I felt my face go red.

Darlene came to my rescue. "Speaking of bras and Robin Hood!" She grabbed Rena's back and snapped. Sure enough, Rena was wearing her much-talked-about bra too! Leave it to Darlene to spot a bra!

After that, I tried to keep my back to the

wall. I wandered over to the refreshment table. I helped myself to some pretzels. My eyes kept drifting to the door, watching. Jeff had not yet arrived.

Sue-Ann spotted him first. He didn't even have a chance to walk in. She was all over him!

"Oh, Jeff, I thought you'd never get here!" she squealed. "Now we'll have some fun at this party!" She hooked her arm through his.

Jeff smiled at me, but I just looked away. He was going to have to make up his mind which one of us he wanted. There was no way I was going to chase him any longer!

I went over to where Lawrence, Harley, Ken, and Marvin were standing in a group. They were looking at something and laughing. It looked interesting.

"What are you guys doing?" I asked.

"We've got a really neat magazine here," Lawrence smirked. "Want to have a look?"

I came closer. It was one of those dirty magazines with pictures of naked girls. They had it opened to the center picture. I had never seen one of those magazines close up. I wasn't sure if I wanted to see one now.

I looked around the room. Jeff was scooping some punch into a cup held by Sue-Ann! I'd show him!

I walked right into the middle of all those boys. "Sure! I'll look at anything you will!"

My eyes bulged. Would I ever look like that? That girl had curves that made Darlene look like Jan Zieglebaum!

"Aw, she's not so great," I lied. "It's disgusting to be so big!"

"Yeah! You wish you were disgusting like that!" Marvin laughed meanly.

Lawrence folded up the magazine. He hid it in a stack of women's magazines from the supermarket. "Let's liven up this party!" he announced to everyone. "How about a little kissing game?"

"How about 'Spin the Bottle'?" Sue-Ann suggested, looking at Jeff.

"That's a baby game. I know a much better one." Lawrence's eyes twinkled.

"What's that" she demanded to know.

"Post Office!" Lawrence smiled sexily.

"How do you play 'Post Office'?" No one else knew either, so Lawrence started to explain.

"It's like this. All the boys get even numbers. The girls get odd. You call out a number. Whoever that is goes with you into the bedroom and delivers the mail."

"Delivers the mail?" Suzy giggled. "What's that?"

"A kiss, dummy. The caller has a choice of regular or special delivery. Here—I'll show you!"

141

Lawrence wrote down numbers on little pieces of paper. Everyone picked one. Mine was number five. Then he went first.

"Number seven," he called out. It was Lisa Finklestein! She smiled and went with him into the bedroom.

"I bet she's going to learn a thing or two," Darlene whispered to me.

We all watched the bedroom door. Sure enough. When they came out again, Lisa had a stunned look on her face.

"Number ten," she called. It was Jeff! I could have died, seeing him go into the bedroom with her! But it was even worse when he called number three and it turned out to be Sue-Ann Fein!

They were in there a long time. When they came out, they were both red-faced. Sue-Ann gave me a big smile as she brushed by me!

I was burning! I could just picture them in the bedroom. Sue-Ann was just the type to push Jeff down on the bed for her kiss.

Lost in gloom, I almost missed my number being called.

"Number five! Where's number five?"

I looked up hopefully. It was Marvin Haven! Just my luck! He was the last person in the world I wanted to kiss!

He closed the bedroom door behind him with a bang. It was dark in there. Only a glint of light shone under the shade. I was glad about that. Maybe I could pretend he was Jeff.

"Well, let's see how I should collect," he asked.

"Huh?"

"You know, regular or special delivery."

"Which is which?"

"Regular is on the cheek, fast. Special delivery is on the lips, slow and deep!"

A sick feeling crept into my stomach. "Why don't we start with regular? We can build up to special delivery later!"

"Well—OK!" He turned his face toward me. I took a deep breath and kissed him as quickly as I could. It was awful!

We went back into the living room. Now it was my turn to call a number. What was Jeff's number? I couldn't believe it! I had completely forgotten!

"Number eight," I guessed. It was Lawrence's number. He strutted toward the bedroom, putting his arm around me as he walked.

He closed the door firmly behind us. "Special delivery, of course."

"Sure." I swallowed hard. I looked up. His dimly-lit face was coming closer to mine. I pursed my lips. His mouth was open!

His lips felt very warm. I could feel his warm breath. He was breathing very hard. His arms pressed me closer.

My heart beat wildly. My eyes were wide open. At least I didn't have to worry about what to do. He was doing all the work!

I relaxed, and it began to feel nice. Grown up. Then—it was over!

I blinked as the living room lights hit my eyes. I sat on the sofa in a daze. So that's what it was like to really be kissed! Now I knew what Darlene meant! I pictured Jeff and me kissing like that. I could feel his lips burning against mine. I forgot the rest of the party.

"Number five! Number five must be asleep!" I opened my eyes. Everyone was looking at me and laughing. I jumped to see who had called my number. It was Jeff!

I walked to the bedroom, still in a daze. I could feel my heart pounding in my chest. It was finally going to happen. I, Linda Berman, member of WHEBB, was about to be kissed by my-own-true-love, Jeff Davidson!

"Watch that the bed doesn't catch on fire!" Lawrence winked as we walked by. I didn't care what he said.

The door slammed. I stood with my back up against it. I needed the support. I didn't say a word.

Jeff didn't either. I could see the faint outline of his face as he stood there. The curls that I loved tumbled over his forehead.

He came closer. Chills went through me. "I

think I'll have a special delivery. May as well get my money's worth!" He laughed nervously.

"OK," I whispered. I waited.

Suddenly, he fell up against me with a bang!

"Hey! Watch out! You're heavy!" I complained.

"Sorry! I tripped," he laughed again. He bent down and kissed me hard on the lips. I had just started to enjoy it when he started laughing again!

I shoved him away. Enough was enough! He hadn't paid attention to me all night, and now this!

"So that's your idea of a special delivery kiss! Well you can just call Sue-Ann's number from now on!"

"Hey, wait a minute!" He was still laughing.

"What?"

"Just this!" He bent down and kissed me again. This time it was a real kiss. It was kind of awkward. It was not as sexy as Lawrence's. But you could tell he meant it.

I closed my eyes and wished it would go on forever. But neither of us knew how to make a kiss last.

"Better?" he asked.

"Much better," I said breathlessly.

I guess we had been in there a long time. When we opened the door to the living room, everyone started clapping. Everyone, that is, but Sue-Ann Fein!

Jeff slipped me a note before we left the party. "Don't read it until you get home," he whispered.

I couldn't wait to open it. I sat on the bed and unfolded it. It was written on a napkin from the party. It said:

> *Open this up and you will see—*
> *That I like you better than Fein,*
> *   really I do.*

I held the note to my beating heart. Finally, I knew the truth. My WHEBB goal had been reached! He really did like me better than Sue-Ann Fein!

In the morning, I gobbled down breakfast. I raced for the park. I couldn't wait to see Jeff again. He smiled and waved when he saw me.

I sat on the wall and watched him play ball. The Royals were playing a new team. These boys looked older. One of them was really cute.

He was short, but very muscular. He was dark, with straight black hair. He flipped his hair back as he ran, but it flopped over his eyes again.

He scooped up the ball in a smooth motion.

He fired it to the third baseman. The runner was out. What an arm! His muscles were so strong!

He opened his mouth to let out a victory yell. His voice broke. It was changing. None of our boys had voices that were changing yet.

"Nice throw, Sheldon!" someone called.

Sheldon! So that was his name. I bet he was at least in ninth grade. I loved the way his voice sounded. I bet he kissed even better than Jeff.

Jeff! I looked to the batter's box. Jeff had just struck out!

For a moment, just for a moment, I had forgotten all about Jeff. How could I do that after last night? I still liked Jeff. I knew I did. But Sheldon was so cute, so mature. Was it possible that someday an older boy like Sheldon would replace my-own-true-WHEBB-love, Jeff Davidson? I guessed I'd just have to wait and find out.

Graduation! We all lined up and filed into the auditorium. We had done this for assembly every week since school had begun. This time it was different.

The boys wore jackets and ties. The girls were all in their pastel graduation dresses.

Instead of the usual kidding around while we lined up, there was solemn silence. As part of the ceremony, we walked into the auditorium holding hands. In the midst of all those graduation dresses, I felt as if I was floating on a bed of pastel flowers.

It was so unreal. This was the very last day of elementary school.

Mr. Wohl gave a speech. I heard his voice booming in my head. I didn't really hear the words. It was something about our being the hope for the future.

We stood up to sing our farewell song:

Farewell to thee,
Three, seven, three,
The time has come to say goodbye; we'll miss
   you.
The school we share.
In your good care,
We leave; so keep it's banner high!

I heard sniffling. I looked around. Almost everyone was crying. Darlene, Suzy, even the boys. All these kids had been with me for so long.

A tear splashed on my dress. Why, I was crying too!

P.S. 373 had been my school for seven years. I remembered starting kindergarten. How scared I had been! I had held on to my mother's hand as tightly as I could.

I had felt safe with her at home. I didn't want to let go of her. I was afraid of the world I didn't know.

Maybe it was the same way now. I didn't want to let go of the school I knew so well. Everything about P.S. 373 was familiar to me. I had my friends; I had WHEBB; I had Jeff. Even Miss Delaney was all right once I got to know her. But I had no idea what lay ahead for me once I left P.S. 373. Miss Delaney, strict as she was, had turned out to be the best teacher I ever had. I had learned so much in her class. P.S. 373 had become almost like home to me. Once I left my school, I had no idea of what lay ahead for me.

I felt a sick feeling in my stomach at the thought. At least if I was going to 515, I would have my friends to count on for help getting through the tough times. Going to Huntington, I'd be on my own. I'd have to grow up fast.

Was I ready?

Closing exercises are over. I'm walking out of the auditorium. No one is holding hands now. I'm walking by myself.

#2 THE SHADOWED PATH
Barbara Corcoran

Sixteen-year-old Phyllis Donahue is alone in her family's remote cabin in the Maine woods. But she is not on her own for long—Ron Harrison, a sophisticated young man, is staying in the next cabin; and strong, quiet David Clark, from a nearby town, promises to visit every day. Phyllis's summer seems to be getting better and better. But then she makes an unsettling discovery, and her isolation develops an undertone of terror. Ron is a tantalizing older boy and something of a "dangerous love." David makes Phyllis feel good inside, but she's not sure he cares. Ron is clearly hiding something, and Phyllis may be playing with fire!

#3 DANGEROUS BEAT
Charlotte Flynn

Seventeen-year-old Jennifer Taggert is thrilled to land a summer job helping the music critic of her town's newspaper. When she meets two attractive, but very different boys, she feels luckier than ever. Billy is the outgoing, adorable blond manager of the local rock-'n-roll group. Ken is moody and distant, but Jennifer is strongly drawn to him. Then important review albums start to disappear at work, and Jennifer realizes that someone is trying to get her fired. She *has* to find out who's causing the trouble, and in the process she comes across a mysterious ice house in the woods, an unexplained death, and a possible rival for Ken's affections. She is determined to pursue the mystery to its end—even if it means losing both boys and endangering her life.

Read on . . .

#4 FATAL SECRETS
Linda A. Cooney

Sixteen-year-old Kate Monroe is excited about getting to know David Pearl, a handsome track star, who is also competing with her in the school science fair contest (with $1000 as the prize). It seems that Kate and David are on the fast track to romance! Then trouble strikes. A puppy is mysteriously poisoned, Kate's science experiment is failing, and David is seen tampering with Kate's best friend's experiment, right before her friend is hospitalized with a mysterious illness. Kate has to find some answers, and David refuses to give them! Her questions may be leading her out of love . . . and into danger.

**Look for MOONSTONE novels
at your local bookstore!**